Cam Reed has found a secret in the Smoky Mountains. The secret's name is Jeddah Whitmire, and everyone thought he was dead.

Jeddah isn't dead, not by a long shot. He's as lively as a pup; as wild and rugged as the mountains themselves. When Cam discovers that Jed has escaped from the local old folks' home run by black marketeer Henry Cawley, he decides to keep the old man's whereabouts to himself. Unfortunately, Cam's determination to save his new friend provokes a family battle, a broken friendship, and the most outrageous church service in the history of Pinehill, North Carolina! As if that weren't enough, rumors about the old tower are starting up again. Is that really where the German spies were headed? Who was the evil-looking man with the black mustache who lived there?

Leonard Todd has written a novel of truth and joyous energy. His beguiling evocation of the Appalachian South creates a time of crazy adventure and vanishing innocence, when everyone could do his bit for the home front—and growing up was the biggest battle of all.

THE BEST KEPT SECRET
OF THE WAR

The
BEST KEPT SECRET
OF THE WAR

Leonard Todd

Alfred A. Knopf
New York

I would like to express my appreciation for the help and encouragement given to me by the Virginia Center for the Creative Arts, the Ossabaw Island Project, and Alfred University Summer Place, where portions of this novel were written. My thanks also go to Galen Williams and the staff of Poets & Writers, Inc.; to Dorothy Pittman, Jane Bloom, and Jeanne Drewsen in New York; to Suzanne St. Clair and Bobbi Thompson in Los Angeles; and to my excellent editors at Knopf, Lori Mack, Doug Hardy, and Pat Ross.

Grateful acknowledgement is expressed to the following for permission to reprint copyrighted material:

Cromwell Music, Inc. for an excerpt from the song "Carolina Moon," Words and Music by Benny Davis and Joe Burke. TRO- © Copyright 1928 and renewed 1956 Cromwell Music, Inc. and Edwin H. Morris & Co., Inc., New York, N.Y. Used by permission.

Holt, Rinehart and Winston, Publishers for an excerpt from *Brave Men* by Ernie Pyle. Copyright 1943, 1944 by Scripps-Howard Newspaper Alliance. Copyright 1944 by Ernie Pyle. Copyright © 1971, 1972 by Holt, Rinehart and Winston. Reprinted by Permission of Holt, Rinehart and Winston, Publishers.

Peer International Corporation for an excerpt from the song "You Are My Sunshine" by Jimmie Davis and Charles Mitchell. Copyright 1940 by Peer International Corporation. Copyright Renewed. Used by Permission. All Rights Reserved.

Library of Congress Cataloging in Publication Data
Todd, Leonard.   The best kept secret of the war.
Summary: During the summer of 1944, ten-year-old Cam Reed fights a few important battles of his own in Pinehill, North Carolina while his daddy is in Europe fighting the Germans. [1. World War, 1939–1945—United States—Fiction. 2. North Carolina—Fiction] I. Title.   PZ7.T56675Be   1984   [Fic]   83-18756
ISBN 0-394-86569-3   ISBN 0-394-96569-8 (lib. bdg.)

*For
my mother
and
my father*

THE BEST KEPT SECRET
OF THE WAR

PARTWAY UP THE MOUNTAIN behind our town, a rock juts out from the forest like a table high in the air. It's wide and flat and worn almost smooth from fathers and sons and their sons who've stood there to look west across the Blue Ridge. They say you can see four states from it—North Carolina close in front, then farther off the mountains of South Carolina, Georgia, and Tennessee running one into the other along the bottom of the sky.

My dad used to stop there with me when we went hiking. We'd sit on the smooth spots and he'd tell me stories about the mountains, and about our family, and about Pinehill down below. We were there when he told me he was going away to war. He told me it was something he had to do. He asked me to take care of Mama while he was gone.

That was more than two years ago. I come back to the rock now whenever I want to think about my father and talk with him in my mind. Sometimes I even pretend I can stare far enough into the horizon to catch a glimpse of him over in Europe. I know I'm looking in the wrong direction, but I can almost see him just the same.

I think of the rock as a special place that belongs only to Dad and me, but that's not true. Other people go there too—professors looking for Indian relics, even picnickers sometimes. Since the war started, though, it's been pretty much forgotten. My friend Talbert Cawley and I seem to be about the only ones who know it still exists. Sometimes we hike up the mountain as fast as we can, racing each other really, to get to the rock. Out of breath and dizzy, we step out of the woods together and onto the stone. We stretch out one arm and hold the other's shoulder to steady ourselves. Laughing, we get as close as we dare to the place where the table breaks off, then ease down on our stomachs and hook our chins over the edge. The whole world, misty and blue, falls away below us.

4

One morning last June we were lying like that on the rock, our shirts pulled up to cool our bellies on the stone. "I bet this is the best view in the Blue Ridge," I said.

"In the whole South," said Tal. There were clouds below us hovering close over Pinehill. We felt like birds gliding slow and smooth through the sky.

"I got a letter from my dad today," I said.

"Oh, yeah? What'd he say?"

I waited a moment to make my answer as dramatic as it deserved to be: "He was part of D-Day. He landed on Normandy."

"Oh," said Tal.

"Well, isn't that great?"

"Yeah," he said, "that's great."

"His division got a good beachhead, and they're already moving inland. Right beside General Omar Bradley. They're gonna drive the Nazis all the way out of France."

Tal didn't take his eyes off the mountains. "Great."

"They're gonna liberate Paris—that's the kind of thing you get medals for."

"I *said* it was great."

Tal can be a very peculiar person. Most times he's a real pal, but every once in a while he goes into a mood. I could tell he was considering one right then. "Hey," I said, trying to be pleasant, "how long you think it'll take 'em to get from Normandy to Paris? Ten days?"

"Damn." He slapped his palms against the stone and pushed himself up onto his knees. "Don't you ever talk about anything but how brave your daddy is?"

"Well, shoot, Tal, I—"

"Just 'cause he's a soldier don't make him so special."

"Yeah, but—"

"A man don't have to wear a uniform to be special. *My* dad don't. President Roosevelt says my dad's so special he needs him right here on the home front."

"I know that." Tal's father has a priority job; he runs an old-age home just outside Pinehill.

"Well, you don't act like you know it. Maybe when you get *older* you will."

If there's anything that makes me mad, it's when Tal starts in about being older than me, and smarter, and bigger. "Twelve's just naturally more advanced than ten," he usually says. And I get furious.

"Well, you may be two years older than me," I said, "but there's one thing I know: all red-blooded American men are in uniform this very minute."

Tal doesn't change his expression much. He has pale hair and pale skin and pale blue eyes that not a lot shows through. He has these long earlobes, though, that get red when he's angry. Right then, they looked like he could start a fire with them. "Come on," he said, his voice low, "I been saving something to show you."

"Uhhh . . . where is it?"

He was on his feet and heading for the woods behind us. "Down Dead End Trail."

"Dead End Trail! But that just comes up to that big old huge ravine. You know we can't get across it."

"You scared to try?"

"Uhhh . . . hell no."

"Then come on."

Now, Dead End Trail Ravine is not the kind of place you mess around with. There are stories about kids trying to get across it and never being heard from again. It's dangerous and crazy to even consider it—just the kind of thing Tal loves. He ran ahead into the woods, swatting at pine boughs. Already regretting it, I got up and followed him.

The trail dropped fast down the mountain, twisting in front of me, and I lost sight of him till I came to the ravine at the end: he was standing on the *other* side, where none of us had ever been before!

"Tal! How'd you you get over there?"

He held out his arm. In his hand was one end of a rope that swept up into an oak tree on my side of the gully. "Simple as pie," he said.

"You *swung* over there?"

"Sure. And it's *your* turn." He sent the rope zooming toward me. I grabbed it with both hands and tried to steady it, but it leaped around like an electric eel. "Well, come on," he said impatiently. "Just get a running start, grab on, and swing across."

Dead End Trail Ravine isn't especially wide, but it is *deep*. I held on to the rope and leaned over to look down into it. It had steep, red clay banks with jagged rocks and rough bushes sticking out of them. The creek at the bottom looked farther away than Tennessee. I could picture myself dropping into the gulch and disappearing forever, just a fossil they'd turn up one day, a fossil at the age of ten. "Tal," I said, "I think I'm too heavy for this rope."

"You *crazy*, boy? It held me, didn't it? And it held Jakie and Rob. We put it up just last week."

"Well, you must've weakened it."

That made him snicker. "Shoot, you're just plain chicken."

"You take that back!" I reached down and scooped up a clod of clay and hurled it at him. He sidestepped it, hardly moving. "Campbell Reed is a chicken," he sang, "who can't even throw straight."

When I missed him again, he came right up to the edge of the ravine. Gravely, he looked me in the eye and said, "So long, chicken-runt." He turned his back and strutted off into the woods.

I stood there feeling awful. I looked up at the rope beside me. I gave it a little shake to test it, but it started weaving like a snake some Indian charmer had left standing in the air. It swayed up as high as the limb, swayed back down, flipped up, and slapped my leg.

I kicked hard at it. I put on all my weight to pull

it down—*that* would fix Talbert Cawley—but it barely shrugged. I let it slip from my hands. Sighing, I started back up the trail for the long walk home by myself. . . .

I stopped dead. On the path in front of me stood the wildest-looking dog I'd ever seen. He was an ugly brown color and fat around the middle. His spine hair was standing on end. His ears were back and he was snarling.

"Ohhh-ohhh, dog!" I held up both hands, but surrendering didn't help. His eyes blazed and he lunged straight for me. I turned on my heels, threw back my head, and lit out. "Help!" I shouted.

In seconds I reached the ravine. Without slowing down, without even thinking, I grabbed the rope. I swung across the creek, forgot to let go on the other side, and came swooping back to where I started. I scrambled higher on the rope, but that only cut short the swing. I came to a flat stop over the dog. He leaped up at me, snapping at my toes.

"*Ta-a-al!*"

Tal came running back to the ravine. "Holy cow!" he cried. He shot into the trees and came out with a long iron rake in his hands. He must've kept it there to recapture the rope when he wanted to get back across. "Now just hang on!" He reached way out and snagged the claws into my backside.

"Ow!" I yelled, wiggling on the rope.

"Hold still, boy! I'm just trying to save your fool

life!" He pulled me toward him, then let go. "Pump!" he shouted.

I pushed my legs in front of me, and he hooked me again. Soon I was swinging wide. "Now *jump!*"

I closed my eyes and let go. I hit the ground rolling, my feet flying over my head. I dug my fingers into the dirt. Even after I came to a stop, the world kept spinning. All I could do was lie there and hold on.

Laughing, Tal dropped to his knees and slapped my back. "You finally did it!"

"N-nothing to it," I said.

The rope was still swinging above the ravine. He jumped up and ran to catch it. Holding it in one hand, he picked up a clod of clay and flipped it across the gulch. It caught the dog on the jaw. "Haw!" he said. He flipped out another.

The dog showed his fangs in the most horrible way. His hackles high, he began to race back and forth.

"Hey, Tal," I said, "you better cut it out." I got to my feet. "You're just making him madder."

"What do we care? Ain't no way he can get to us."

"Yeah—but he might try real hard."

"Just *let* him."

Almost as if he understood what we were saying, the dog gave us a bloodcurdling look and began to pick his way down the bank. "See?" I said. "Come on, we better get out of here."

"You still chicken? He'll never make it to the bottom." With that, the dog lost his footing and slid on his side all the way down the bank and into the creek. He jerked himself up, shook off, and kept coming. Tal hooted but looked a little nervous. "He'll never make it up this side." He had both hands on the rope now.

I leaned out to look down into the gulch. There were so many bushes and rocks that I couldn't see the dog anymore. I leaned out a little farther. All of a sudden, a snout poked up right below me. The dog was snuffling and scratching up the bank like a wolf out for blood.

"Outta my way!" I shouted. I leaped for the rope, but Tal was quicker. He jerked up his feet and swept off for the other side. He'd gone so white he looked like a big piece of chalk swinging from a string. Before he even touched down, the dog heaved up over the edge of the bank, ready to kill.

I took off, any direction, just off. Crashing into the woods, I stumbled onto a trail. I tore down it, hoping maybe the dog wasn't after me at all—Tal was bigger, more meat on his bones—but when I heard leaves bashing behind me, I understood I was the main course on the menu.

I raced along like I was blind. The only thing that got through to me was that I was on one of the hills at the base of the mountain. I realized I'd come there before but from a different direction, from across the dam down by Davis Pond. And then I remembered: an old cabin was stuck out somewhere in these woods, probably along this trail. If I could get to it, and if it wasn't too tumbled down . . .

Fear is supposed to make you strong, but I was ready to drop in my tracks. I was wheezing like a broken accordion. In another minute I'd be completely out of breath. The dog seemed to know that. He closed the distance between us little by little, ready for me to fall.

The trail took a sharp jog into a clearing. I saw the cabin straight ahead. An old man was sitting on the front steps. He looked in worse shape than the shack, but he was a human being, somebody to help me.

"Look out!" I yelled, dashing across the clearing. I caught my foot on a root, went sprawling, slid along the ground right up to the steps. I rolled over and saw the old man sitting just above me. He seemed half asleep. Dreamily, he held out his hand like a stop sign for the dog.

That grisly animal, that hungry wolf, skidded up to a halt. He got this bashful expression on his face, as if the whole thing had been a joke. He looked up at the old man and wagged his tail!

They stared at each other, the old man dreamy, not saying a word, the dog wiggling and trying to apologize. I figured they were both crazy.

Slowly I eased up. Trying not to breathe, I moved off toward the woods. The dog growled, low and mean, but didn't come after me.

At the trees, I threw a quick glance back at the old man. He wasn't watching me. He was staring off into nowhere, as if he'd never even known I was there.

C HARLIE," SAID TAL, "THAT dog coulda eaten Cam in one bite!" We were talking to Charlie Cogswell in his grocery store. "He was big and fat and tall up to *here.*"

"And his teeth were *this* long," I said, "and his eyes looked like this." I screwed my face into the most gruesome expression I knew.

"Lord," said Charlie, "that musta been some terrible animal." He stuck his pencil behind his ear and propped his elbows on the counter. He's got a wide, friendly face, and everybody in Pinehill likes him. The only odd thing about him is his hair. It's thin on top and real thick on the sides. To make it look even, he lets one side grow long and then combs it across to meet the other half. It looks fine when he opens the store at eight A.M., but by ten each morning the long half is flapping out over his ear like an awning. He's over fifty years old, but when he gets interested in something and his hair starts flopping, he looks about nine. "Were you scared, Cam?"

I started to say, "Well, yeah, but not too scared." Tal jumped in before I had the chance and said, "Was he scared? He just about peed in his pants! Scared? Haw, I never seen anybody so scared."

"*Me* scared?" I said right back. "*You* were so scared you flew off like a turkey."

"Oh, yeah?"

"Yeah. *I'm* the one who was courageous enough to stick around and face that dog single-handed. Leading him off like I did—swinging back through the trees, hand over hand, till he lost my scent."

I know it didn't happen quite that way. But Tal had started kidding me as soon as I got back to the ravine, saying how ridiculous I looked hightailing it across the countryside with that dog on my heels, so I had to make up something that sounded better than the truth: that a feeble old man just held up his hand and the dog started wagging his tail!

Charlie listened to us go at it. "Yes, sir," he said, "that musta been some terrible animal. Matter of

---

15

fact, it sounds like the one I saw scrounging 'round my store yesterday. But that wasn't no he. That was a she-dog."

"How do you know that?" I said.

"How do I know! Cam, that dog was carrying a litter of pups in her belly. That's how I know."

Tal and I stared at each other. *That's* why that dog was so fat.

"Yep," said Charlie, "I can see we must be talking 'bout the same animal. Poor miserable thing. She's old as the hills and hungry and having puppies again. Ain't no wonder she's mean."

"Don't she belong to somebody?" said Tal.

"More'n likely not. Dogs get lost in these mountains when they're pups, and they just wander 'round their whole lives trying to keep body and soul together. How they get through the winter is beyond me." He tapped the counter with the palm of his hand and shook his head. "Well, anyway . . . what can I do for you? Your folks send you over for some canned goods?"

"Naw," said Tal, "we just wanted to tell you about that dog."

"And, oh, yeah," I said, "I wanted to tell you Mama and I heard from Daddy."

"You *did?* Is he all right? Was he in on D-Day like we figured?"

I sucked in my breath. "Yep, he sure was. And he's just fine."

"That Pat Reed!" said Charlie. "Always leading the way! Lemme move his flag. Lemme move it right now."

Charlie has this giant map of the world on the wall of his store. He has little flags and ships and strings stuck all over it so he can follow everything that happens in the war. There's a flag on a pin for General Eisenhower and one for General MacArthur and one for each of the Pinehill men in the service. There's even a black one with a swastika on it for Hitler in Berlin.

Charlie's had the map ever since the day after the attack on Pearl Harbor. That day he got in his car and drove up to the recruiting office in Asheville and then on over to the one in Charlotte, but at both places they told him that fifty was just too old to go to war. He tried every argument he knew, till they practically had to throw him out and lock the door. When he finally realized he'd have to spend the war on the home front, he went to a bookstore in Charlotte and bought the bigget map of the world they had in stock. He brought it back here, nailed it up, and put a scroll over it that said "The Fighting Men of Pinehill, N.C., Around the World." He even stuck a flag for himself on it, right over Pinehill, that said "HQ" for Headquarters. Some people say that's kind of peculiar, but I don't think so. I wish he'd put one for me on there too.

Charlie pulled the flag with "Sgt. P. B. Reed" on

it out of England and moved it over to the coast of France. "Yes, sir," he said, "that Pat is leading the way."

"I know it," I said. "He sure is."

Rubbing his chin, Charlie stared at the map. "Lotta work needs to be done to bring this document up to date." He looked at me and raised his eyebrows. "What do you say, Cam? You up to it?"

"Sure!"

Charlie decides to overhaul the map about once a week, always on the spur of the moment. Sometimes he won't let anybody else touch it; you have to stand back and watch. Today was different. Laying out the Asheville paper to refer to, he told me and Tal how to shift around the ships and pins ourselves.

There were things to be done in Italy and out in the Pacific, but the most exciting changes were in France: the little red string that showed the front lines was inching toward Paris. And Daddy's flag was right behind it.

For me, working on the map was a real honor, but Tal put down the pins after a few minutes and walked to the screen door. He opened it and stood there like he was hoping I'd go with him. He said, "Well . . . I'll see you."

I said, "Don't you want to stay a while, Tal?"

"No."

"Okay, so long." I watched him amble down the porch steps and off along the road. I could never figure him out. One minute he'd be happy like every-body else, the next he'd be bullying me into risking my neck. And then he'd slouch off like the loneliest boy in the world.

Charlie handed me a cutout of a destroyer. "This goes in the Atlantic Ocean," he said, "wherever you can find room." He stood back and surveyed the battle lines. "That Pat! When exactly did he get the word, Cam? About the invasion and all."

I picked up a carrot from the fresh produce bin. Using it for a pointer, I tapped the map. "What he said in his letter, Charlie, is that all our soldiers over in England"—I pointed to London—"knew they'd be part of an invasion of Europe. But it wasn't till they were actually sailing up to France that they found out they were gonna land in Normandy. Right over here."

Charlie already knew this from the radio, but he got excited about it all over again. "No! A secret right till the last minute?"

"Yep. Daddy says it was the best kept secret of the war. And he says there were so many ships you could hardly see the water. More ships, he said, than at any other time in history."

Charlie had to sit down when he heard that. "In all of recorded history," he said. "Right here in our time—on the sixth of June, Nineteen Hundred and Forty-four. And we had a representative from Pine-hill right there." He got wet-eyed and had to blow his

---

19

nose. "And the important thing, Cam, is that he came through safe and unharmed. That's the important thing."

"There's something else. He got promoted to master sergeant."

"Promoted!" Charlie leaped up and slammed his hand against his leg. "Lord, boy, how could you keep something like that to yourself?" He went straight to the list of Pinehill men by the map and started erasing Daddy's old rank. " 'Master Sergeant Patrick Bethune Reed.' What a fine ring that's got to it. Now, I gotta cut out his new insignia and paste it up here . . . and then I oughta make a new flag for him too."

"Can I come help you with it tomorrow, Charlie?" I couldn't stay much longer; I had to get to my aunt Eulalee's for lunch.

"Sure, course you can. We got a lot to do to bring this map right up to the minute. Come any time."

"Okay."

"And listen," he said, putting his hand on my shoulder, "tell your mama I'm mighty proud of Pat, hear?"

"I sure will."

"Mighty proud."

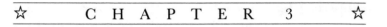

ORE SHIPS THAN AT ANY
time in the history of the world!

I walked along picturing how they must have
looked. I tried to imagine them gathered here, cover-
ing all this part of North Carolina—destroyers and
transports and battleships and cruisers, one after the
other. I could see them riding these hills like they
rode the waves.

I came to the trees at the edge of Aunt Eulalee's

property. Her house sits far back from the road, along the top of a meadow. For a moment it looked like a ship to me, locked way up here in the mountains.

I guess it is a ship, in a way. It was built by my great-great-great grandfather Lucius Bethune, from Charleston, who grew up as a cabin boy on the Mississippi. When he came to build the house, he made it look as much like a steamboat as possible—with long double-decker verandas and railings, everything but a paddle wheel. He even framed the upper porch in arches made out of latticework. He wanted to call it the Delta Queen, but his wife, Loti Lowndes Bethune, said that wasn't dignified. All those arches made it look more like a garden house, she said. She named it the Arbor.

The Arbor was the first big house in this section. It was used only in the summer back then, when Lucius and Loti would come up to get away from the heat down in Charleston. They'd bring all their servants and children and friends. Everybody who visited liked it so much up here that before long about twenty other Charleston families built summer houses too. They built a store—the one Charlie has now—and a chapel, and they called it all Pinehill.

There never has been any *town* in Pinehill, just a collection of these big white wooden houses along the road, each one way off to itself behind the trees. Driving through on the highway, all you see is a sign that says "You Are Entering Historic Pinehill" and another one two miles later that says you're leaving. I guess it was all pretty fancy up till the Civil War. Since then, nobody's had the money to keep the houses up like they should be, and most of them are about ready to fall apart.

Eulalee lived alone in the Arbor for years after her husband, Uncle Jonathan Bethune, died. When Daddy got his orders from the army, though, she came by our house and said she wanted Mama and me to move in with her. She said Pat was her only nephew, like her only child really. With him going to war, the rest of us ought to stick close together.

Daddy closed our house and moved our things to the second floor of the Arbor. I have a big bedroom to myself there that opens right onto the upstairs porch. The place is pretty rundown, but I'd rather live there than just about anywhere, at least until he comes home.

I walked up the clay drive to the house. I could smell lunch cooking. I bounded up the steps and into the front hall. I followed my nose through the big rooms to the kitchen. "I'm home."

Eula turned around and looked at me like I was a missing person. "Lord, child," she said, "where you been? Can't anybody get to the table on time around here?" Eula's bony and tall. She wears her gray hair piled on top of her head so she can be even taller. She makes a big point of towering over anybody she disapproves of. I walked up and let her tower over me. "Lyda," she called, "bring it on! He's here."

"When it's *ready,* Miss Eu'lee," called back Lyda

from the stove. Lyda's worked for Eula longer than I've been alive, and she does pretty much what she wants. "When it's ready, I'll *bring* it."

"Lord, all right. Just hurry it along. Now, where's Miss Bess?"

"She ain't down yet," said Lyda.

"Not *down* yet?" Flaring her nose, Eula went to the kitchen door. "Bess?" she shouted. "Lunch is ready. You planning to stay upstairs all day?"

"I'll go get her," I said.

"No," said Eula, pushing me into a chair at the kitchen table. "If she's gonna be late, she's gonna be late. Bring it on, Lyda."

Lyda bustled up with two steaming plates. "Mind your fingers, Mr. Cam," she said. "They hot."

The kitchen door swished open and Mama came in. She was wearing a white skirt and a blouse with yellow flowers on it. She'd just brushed her hair and put on fresh lipstick. She looked real nice. "Hi, Mama."

"Time just got away from me," she said, patting me on the shoulder. "But here I am."

"Well, we're waiting on you like one mule waits on another," said Eula. "Have some lima beans. We already helped ourselves."

"My, they look good."

"One thing we have at the Arbor," said Eula, "war or no war, is good vegetables. I don't know why the newspapers think victory gardens are something new. Jonathan and I always had one, and I always will."

"Well, I guess they're new for people who live in cities," said Mama, helping her plate. "I hear they're growing corn in the middle of Atlanta. In between all those tall buildings."

"Is that right, Mama?"

"It must be. I heard it from Aunt Roselle."

"Oh!" said Eula. She raised both hands and motioned for us not to say another word till she finished chewing what was in her mouth. She took a gulp of iced tea, swallowed hard, and said, "In the excitement of getting Pat's letter this morning, I forgot to tell you—Roselle wrote us too. Run to the front hall, Son, and get it!"

Roselle is Eulalee's favorite sister. Next to the radio, she's our main contact with what's going on in the world. Living in Birmingham, Alabama, where the steel mills are and where so many soldiers are stationed, she can see exactly what the war is doing to the home front. She passes on every detail to us: nobody going to church anymore, people living in chicken coops because of the housing shortage, men hoarding goods and selling them for a fortune on what they call the black market—morals just falling to pieces. After every letter we sit back and say, "*What* is this world coming to?"

I hurried back from the hall and handed the letter to Eula. "Now, y'all go on and eat while I read," she said, tearing it open. "Roselle's always good mealtime entertainment. Here's what she writes:

> "Dear Loved Ones,
>
> I hope all of you are well and that you have nothing but good news from Pat. A lot of fine boys are in the service, but he is special!
>
> I am getting along okay here in Birmingham, except that I am just *sick* over something I heard last night from my friend Florence. It is about a saboteur, but not the kind we are used to. No, this one is *thirteen years old!* Just a boy!
>
> The authorities won't reveal his name, but this much we do know: one night last week that little devil got hold of a *stick of dynamite,* crept down to the railroad tracks, stuck it under the rails, and lit the fuse! Thank the Lord, he did not know you have to attach a cap. Later, when the police got him, he said he was trying to cut off all roads into town—so he could set himself up as *dictator!*
>
> Can you imagine? It looks like we not only have Hitler to worry about now but thirteen-year-old boys too!!"

Eula looked up with eyes as big as the plates on the table. "Isn't that the worst thing you've ever heard of? A boy saboteur!" She turned to me like I had a bomb up in my closet and said, "Don't you get any ideas, you hear?"

"I don't wanta be no dictator," I said.

She clucked her tongue. "Well, see that you *don't.*" She turned the page, and pieces of newspaper fell out. "Oh, look! Roselle cut out some things for us. One for you, Bess . . . that she says will help you bear up under the strain of Pat being gone . . . and Ernie Pyle's column for you, Cam."

Ernie Pyle is a newspaper correspondent who writes home about the war. This column looked like it was on the invasion of France. I stuck it in my pocket for later, when I could enjoy it alone.

Mama didn't seem very excited about hers. "It's just another one of those things that says 'Wives at home must learn to endure.' " She tossed it onto the shelf behind the table. "Honestly, I wish somebody'd write something that said 'Forget the war for a while. Kick up your heels!' That's what I'd like to read."

"Why, Bess," said Eula, "it's the duty of a soldier's wife to—"

"Oh, Eula, I know all about duty. That's all anybody talks about these days. And I'm *glad* to do my duty. Lord knows I've done my share of worrying. I'd just like to have a little *fun* once in a while too."

"So would everybody," said Eula. "But wartime is just not the time for fun."

"Well, it sure would help. I mean I've just worried about Pat till I—sometimes I think I'll go crazy if I worry any more."

Eula patted her hand. "No, you won't, Bess. We're all here to help each other through this."

Mama sighed and picked at her lima beans. She turned to me. "Cam, did *you* have any fun this morning?"

"Well, I was down at Charlie's store," I said, "to let him know about Daddy. And he said to tell you he was mighty proud. And, oh, yeah, I almost got eaten by a mad dog."

"A mad dog!" said Mama and Eula together. "What are you saying, Son?"

"Well, maybe not a *mad* dog—but the meanest, ugliest one you've ever seen. It was *this* high, and it had eyes like—" Before I could show what a disgusting creature it was, a loud crunch came from the front yard and somebody yelled, "Jee-*hosh*aphat!"

"What in the world?" said Eula.

I got up and hurried to the front porch. A shiny black car, big as a tank, was sitting in the driveway. One wheel was hanging over into the little pool that the drive circles around in front of the steps. Henry Cawley was standing beside the car looking down at the wheel. He was saying "Jee-*hosh*aphat" every two seconds. Tal stood right next to his daddy, acting just as mad.

Even though Tal always does everything his father does, they don't look much alike. Mr. Cawley is dark and beginning to be thick through the middle.

He has long earlobes like Tal, but his are furry. None of the other men in Pinehill wear suits except on Sunday, but Mr. Cawley wears one every day of the week. It's always the same one, with gray stripes. It's getting a little thin at the elbows.

Eula and Mama came up behind me. "What happened, Henry?"

"It's plain, ain't it?" He flopped his hand toward the pool, showing off a big square cufflink at his wrist. "This pool is a *menace.* Right here in the middle of the drive like it is."

"Nobody ever ran into it before," said Eula.

"Nobody ever had a new Packard before! Cars are bigger now, Mrs. Bethune. They take up more space. You're just gonna have to modernize." He kicked at the row of bricks around the pool like they were the most old-fashioned things he'd ever seen.

"Yeah," said Tal. "My daddy's got enough to worry about—what with old Jeddah and all."

"Jeddah Whitmire?" said Eula. "What about Jeddah?"

"Hush up, Son," said Cawley. "I'll tell that part." Getting polite, he came up to the bottom of the steps. "In all this upset, Mrs. Bethune, I didn't even get a chance to say a decent hello." He raised his hat. "And to you, too, Bess. You're looking mighty pretty in those yellow flowers."

"Oh, thank you, Henry," said Mama. "I love your car. Did you just get it?"

"Just this morning. Yes, I did."

"It's the newest one in Pinehill," said Tal.

"Now, Son, no need to blow our own horn." He chuckled at his joke and patted Tal on the back.

"Well, what is it you got to tell us about Jeddah?" said Eula.

Mr. Cawley dusted off his hat. "I'm afraid my news is not good. Old Jeddah Whitmire has been living up at the Cawley Home for the Aged for a number of years. And though we loved him as best we could, he just never quite fit in."

"We know he's in the Home, Henry," said Eula. "Now what's the news?"

"Well, I ought to tell you first that he has not been of sound mind for some time. The first sign was when he started accusing me of not delivering letters from his daughter—but the dire truth is his daughter had *died*, and we were sparing him the news. Every day his condition worsened. He began to lose the gift of speech. I had Dr. Simpson look at him, and we all agreed his mind was rotted. Totally. When last I saw him, he couldn't say one word."

"When *I* last saw him," said Eula, "he was bright as a dollar."

"Ah yes, Mrs. Bethune, but that was no doubt several months ago. At his age the brain rots mighty fast. The tragic upshot of it all is that this morning about nine o'clock we went to get him and found him *gone*. Disappeared, we think, through a break in the fence. Just wandered off with that senile brain of his."

I got all excited—it sounded like the old man in the woods. "What did he look like, Mr. Cawley?"

He ignored me. "Yes, I've done everything I know—had Sheriff Dupree and his deputies out all over the county—but we haven't found hide nor hair of him. So I am alerting all Pinehillians to keep an eye out, just in case."

"What did he *look* like?" I said again.

"If you don't mind," said Mr. Cawley, clearing his throat and looking at me like I was some kind of bug, "we grownups are trying to have a discussion."

"Yeah," said Tal. He crossed his arms and leaned back against his daddy's new car.

Ohhh-kay.

Okay, I'll be quiet. Even though I'm the only one in Pinehill who knows where Jeddah Whitmire is.

I guess it'll just have to be a secret.

A war secret.

L̷ORD, BOY," SAID EULA,
"you sticking like glue this afternoon."

I'd followed her into the front parlor after lunch.
It's just across the entrance hall from the living room.
Since her bedroom is right behind it, she considers it
her own special area. She likes to sit there and read
mystery novels. Mama once tried to get her to read
Gone with the Wind because it was more uplifting, but
she said Scarlett O'Hara didn't interest her half as
much as Agatha Christie.

"Yes'm."

"Well . . . long as you're here, draw up a chair."

I sat down in one of the big upholstered rockers she keeps by her reading table. On the table were her books. They had gory pictures on the jackets—daggers and revolvers and bottles of poison. "Don't these give you the willies?" I said.

"Course they do. That's what they're supposed to do."

That stumped me. I spent half my time trying *not* to get the willies. "Uh, Eula?" I said.

"Yes?"

"Mr. Cawley was talking about that old man from the Home . . . ?"

"Jeddah Whitmire?"

"That's right. Well, you knew him when he was young, didn't you?"

She looked at me with astonishment. "I most certainly did not!" she said. "Why, Jeddah Whitmire is my *father's* age. How old do you think I am, child?"

"No, Eula," I said, patting the air to calm her down. "I just meant what was he like when you were a little girl?"

"Well, that's *different.*" She propped an arm on one of her books. "Let's see," she said. "The first time I saw Jeddah I was about five years old. He was probably around thirty then. He was good looking—tall, with curly sandy-colored hair and a big mustache and the brightest two eyes I'd ever seen. He could make me laugh like nobody else. He'd sit in the swing and carry on with my doll just like she was alive. Jeddah Whitmire—just his name used to start me smiling."

She sighed and began to tidy up the table between us. "When I was about ten," she said, "he went down to the coast for a few years. When he came back, he seemed twenty years older. He'd been through some hard times. The gas station he'd bought had gone broke, and the girl he'd married had died. And, of course, he had that daughter of his hanging on to him." She scowled. "That daughter! Hmh!"

"What did she do, Eula?"

"Never cared about anybody but herself, for one thing. Spent all the money she could lay her hands on, for another. And soon as she could wangle it, she married a rich man up in New Jersey—a lingerie manufacturer, of all people." She shook her head. "Clara Louise Whitmire was *not* a good daughter. Still, poor Jeddah loved her more than anything. He used to tell me he was saving his money to go live with her in his old age. Instead, she puts him in the Cawley Home. In Cawley's! It makes my blood boil just to think about it. And *then* she ups and *dies*. No wonder Jeddah quit talking."

"Is it terrible up there in the Home?"

"Oh, Henry keeps everything just perfect, I suppose. Still, every one of those old people feels forgotten. Most of the time it can't be helped; their families can't keep them for one reason or another. And they try to make the best of it. But how can you go on living a full life when there's no need for you anymore? The ladies up there don't even sew—'cause nobody wants what they make."

"Well, maybe Mr. Cawley could help 'em start a store or something."

"Not Henry. I tried to get him to plant a vegetable garden for them to work in, but he said it would spoil the look of the lawn. I brought them a big basket of novels, but he said mysteries clouded the brain. No, everybody just sits around up there with nothing to do—all the juice gone from their lives. Just waiting to die."

I pictured the old people rocking silently together. "It must be terrible," I said finally, "to be old."

"Don't look at *me* when you say that."

"You're not old, Eula."

"No, honey, but it won't be very long before I am. And if it wasn't for you and your mama I'd be alone too. All alone in this big old house without anybody to even say 'scuse me to." She balled her fist and bounced the soft part of it against the table. "Well . . . listen at me, already feeling sorry for myself. If I get to be that kind of old lady, Cam, the kind that whines all the time, you just roll me up one of these mountains and dump me off the other side." She tapped my arm. "You do it, you hear?"

"First thing in the morning."

Laughing, she shooed me out of the parlor. I got some iced tea from Lyda and went out to the back yard. I walked up the slope past the toolshed to the orchard. It covers the whole hillside behind the house. I bent down a limb and examined the new apples. They were hard little knots now, but when fall came they'd be some of the best in this area. Bethune apples are almost famous around here.

Eula and Uncle Jonathan used to run the orchard together when he was alive. Now she has a family named Connestee to manage it for her. She says it brings in just enough cash to keep herself and the Arbor from going to ruin.

I sat down in the shade of one of the trees. Normally my mind would just drift off. This afternoon, though, I thought hard about Jeddah Whitmire: I was the only person who knew he was out there in that cabin, and if I didn't tell anybody, and he *died* or something . . .

On the other hand, I'd seen the Cawley Home for the Aged. It was big and gray, with a fence around it that was carefully hidden in the forest. I know Eula said Mr. Cawley kept it nice, but to me it looked about as friendly as a penitentiary. Maybe that's what it was for Jeddah Whitmire. Maybe he didn't just wander off, maybe he *escaped*.

I'd never actually been inside the building—no children were allowed, not even Tal; he and his father lived in the director's cottage at the edge of the property—but I'd heard tales about it all my life. They were as terrible as anything in a mystery novel. According to the stories, the house was built by a Yankee millionaire who came down to Pinehill in the 1890s. He built it in the shape of an Alpine mansion, with porches and balconies and big gabled roofs. Up above the rear wing he added a wooden tower, round and pointed. The tower had only one room in it and one window. No one knew what the tower was for until one awful night a year after the house was finished. That night, as usual, the millionaire and his wife dressed for dinner. She put on a long black velvet gown. As she walked into the dining room, she suddenly twitched her head like she'd had a spasm in her neck. Her eyes got huge. She pointed straight in front of her and began to shriek about skeletons and bones and skulls. They were in that house, she screamed, and they were coming for her.

The millionaire grabbed her and carried her upstairs. She fought but he took her all the way up to the room at the top of the tower and locked her in. She screamed there for the whole night, clawing at the walls, loud enough to put the fear of God into everybody for miles. The next morning she was all right, and he let her out. Till the next time, and the next. . . .

In 1915 the millionaire and his wife both died suddenly and mysteriously. The rumor was that she poisoned their food. The place went up for sale, but nobody in his right mind would buy it after all that had happened. The state finally took it over and converted it into an insane asylum. When screams shot out of it again, everybody said it seemed like old times.

There was a big scandal in 1922 about the guards chaining up the inmates in the tower, so the government closed the place down. It was deserted for about ten years. During that time only a few people were brave enough—dumb enough—to crawl in through the windows and climb up the dusty stairs to the room at the top of the tower. There they found the bones of crazy people still chained to the walls, the same bones the millionaire's wife had foreseen, skeletons that moved and walked and crushed to pieces anybody who came near them. One man, Charlie Cogswell's cousin, lost the feeling in both hands after glimpsing the inside of that room. Another packed his bags and left town forever.

Tal's father came to Pinehill in the early 1930s and bought the house for practically nothing. He closed off half of it, including the tower, and turned the rest into the Cawley Home for the Aged, "Blessed Abode in the Blue Ridge." Blessed or not, it never drew more than about twenty residents at one time. As soon as they got in, they wanted to get out. If I'd been Mr. Whitmire, living with that evil tower looking down on me, I'd have gotten out too. Especially if I couldn't talk . . . couldn't even call for help when those bones started bearing down on me. . . .

"Boo."

My scalp jumped. Tal was leaning against a tree, grinning at me. "You look like you just seen a ghost."

"Oh, hey . . . whew, yeah, I was thinking about —uh, just things."

He dropped down beside me. "What things?"

"Oh . . . just those stories about the tower over at the Home. Don't you ever worry? I mean, you live so close to it."

"You mean the skeletons and all?"

"Yeah."

He hunched his shoulders and shivered. "Only in the night . . . when I'm lying in my bed alone and the wind's howling outside. And I hear this 'clink-clunk-clink' coming closer and closer. And this cold mist fills my lungs like the Breath of Death. . . . That's the only time I worry."

"Great day, Tal! I'd do more worrying than that. What if you wake up *dead* one morning?"

He chuckled. "Son, you are some chicken. You look just like you did when you were running from that dog." He lay back on the ground and rolled his head in satisfaction. "Yep, scared of a poor old pregnant dog. Guess you thought that meant a whole posse of dogs was after you."

"I wasn't so scared."

"You were pee-in-your-pants scared. Of a dog having puppies!"

"She was no such a thing! I don't care what Charlie says."

"Don't you know a pregnant dog when you see one? Don't you know the facts of life? Shoot, boy."

"Shoot yourself! I know all about the damn facts of life."

"Oh, yeah? Then why'd you say she wasn't pregnant?"

I was in a corner. "Uh, hell, I just wanted to find out if *you* knew the facts of life."

"Course I know. Damn right I do."

"Prove it."

He looked at me like I'd just said the most ridiculous thing in history. *"Prove* it?"

"Yeah, prove it."

He stretched his arms and sucked on a tooth. "You probably wanta know real bad, don't you?" He smiled, almost to himself. Finally he said, "Hell, all right. I'll help you out." He rolled over onto his belly. "It's like this: men and women are different from each other."

"I *know* that."

"Well, you gotta know that to begin with. 'Cause the woman hasn't got a peter, see, like you and me, she's got this . . . this . . ."

"Yeah, sure, I know, a hole."

"Yeah, right, a hole—and that's where the baby comes out when it's born."

Now that particular part of it had never occurred to me, but I said, "Sure, right through the hole. Right on out."

"Damn right," he said. "I'm glad you know *some* things, son. Course you don't know the main thing, 'bout how the baby gets started. Too bad you don't know the main thing. That's what you asked me, ain't it—how do babies get started? Ain't that what you said? Huh?"

There wasn't much I could do, just look bored and lie like crazy. "Hell, I know that part too."

"Nooo," he said, "that's what you asked me. That's what you said—'Where do babies come from?'—and you're lucky I'm older and know things like that and got the time to teach you. Damn lucky." He pulled in a deep breath and looked important. "Okay. Here it is: the baby starts in the middle of the woman's stomach. And the way it *gets* started is her husband takes her to the doctor. The doctor lies her down, and then he gives her a shot. Right in the bellybutton."

"A *shot?*" I said. "Why does he do that?"

"To start the baby, that's why. Don't you know anything? He sticks the needle in her bellybutton— she don't even feel it—and he shoots in this chemical. And that starts the baby growing inside."

My flesh crawled just to think about it. "That don't sound right," I said.

"What don't?"

"The shot part. That don't sound right."

"Yeah? Well, Mr. Smart-Runt, what do *you* think happens?"

"Well ..." I searched for inspiration. "I think the woman lies down ... she lies down, and then her husband kisses her. ..." I concentrated. "And then real carefully he spits in her mouth, and that starts the baby."

"*Spi-its!*" Tal rolled over onto his back, shouting it out, his feet in the air. "You think you started from a wad of *spit?*"

I jumped up, embarrassed at thinking up such a dumb idea, furious at Tal for making me do it. "I didn't come from a stupid old *vaccination,* like you did." I kicked his butt as hard as I could. "You needlehead!" I stalked off, leaving him laughing on the ground.

"*You're* the needlehead!" he yelled between heehaws.

"Yeah?" I shouted, whirling back at him. "Oh, *yeah?* Well, you—you're nothing but a—a *boy saboteur!*" It was the worst thing I could think of.

"A *what* ... ?"

I pointed a finger straight at him. "My aunt Roselle wrote us about a kid like you who tried to blow up a railroad. He was a boy saboteur—and that's what *you* are!"

"Why'd he wanta blow up a train?"

"Because he was mean and stupid and wanted to be a dictator, that's why!"

Tal probably didn't like the stupid part, but the mean dictator seemed to suit him just fine. He dropped back his head and went on chuckling.

I STOOD UNDER THE ARCHES on the upstairs porch and watched the rain clouds gather. They congregate in the peaks above Pinehill almost every afternoon, usually about six o'clock, then skim down the mountain, roll across Eulalee's yard, and crash into the house. Ambushed, they break open with rain.

I looked along the porch and tried to figure how many rain clouds had collided with it since it was built: one a day for almost a hundred years.

The Arbor has held up pretty well, considering all the storms and wars it's been through. Still, the roof leaks, and the arches are losing their white paint, and the tapestries that hang in the stairwell are full of moth holes. The piano is out of tune, and the chandelier in the front hall is missing half its prisms. Eula calls it all "faded Bethune glory."

Almost every piece of furniture in the house has been here since Loti Lowndes Bethune first furnished it. She and Lucius went to Europe and brought back a whole shipload of things—oriental carpets, yellow marble mantelpieces, mahogany chairs, a dining table long enough to seat every one of her summer visitors. She covered the walls with silk and filled the hall cabinets with gold-rimmed dishes and crystal bowls. She hung an oil painting of a different European city in every room, like big postcards from her trip. Eula keeps up what's left because Uncle Jonathan loved it, but every few weeks, usually at housecleaning time, she threatens to move to the Blue Ridge Motel and just let the whole place disintegrate.

If she does, there's one piece of it I want her to save: the marble statue that stands in the little circular pool in the driveway. I could see it from where I was standing on the porch. It's the figure of a girl getting ready to go in swimming. Her clothes are bunched up around her ankles, she hasn't got a stitch on, and you can see everything. She's not trying to cover up, not even the part between her legs. It's there in plain sight. You don't find much of that around Pinehill, so I figure she's worth saving.

She's the main reason I know what I know about women. "Men and women are different," Tal says. Of course I know that. All I have to do is look at her and see that. But the rest of it . . . not spit . . . but not a shot in the bellybutton either.

A big drop of rain splashed into the water beside the girl. I looked up and saw the clouds moving in fast. The chairs at the other end of the porch began to rock. The lattices above me were already damp. In a minute the mist would be deep over us.

I thought about poor Mr. Whitmire out there in the forest. I hoped he had sense enough to get inside the cabin. He was probably wandering around getting soaked. Just him and that dog of his.

I remembered the time Daddy and I got caught out in a storm together, way out in a field. I was little then and scared because it came on all of a sudden with lightning and thunder. Daddy said, "A little water won't hurt us, huh, Cam?" but I started crying and wanted to hide under a tree. He picked me up and put me on his shoulders. He carried me along, saying, "If we keep walking, Son, we'll pass right through it." The rain poured down on us; flashes jittered all around; thunder boomed on top. I'd never heard anything so loud in my life. Daddy told me not to be afraid, that it was only the Devil bowling up in the sky, knocking down giant tenpins. "He's swing-ing," he said. "It's rolling—hear it?—*boom!*"

I held on to his forehead, frightened of the noise even if it was just the Devil. I tried to bury my face down deep in his wet hair. He held his hands around my arms, awfully tight, and I wondered for a terrible moment if he was afraid too. The loudest crash of all came, and suddenly I heard him singing above it:

> *"You are my sun-shine,*
> *My only sun-shine,*
> *You make me hap-pee*
> *When skies are gray!"*

He shouted it out—"You are my sunshine!"—and I knew we must be all right. We were soaking wet, holding tight, but we were outyelling the Devil. "Sing, Cam!" he shouted, and I did: "Please don't ta-a-ke my sun-shine away. . . ."

The clouds broke open now. I put my hands on the porch railing and watched the drops collect on my knuckles. They hung for only a second, then let go and plummeted toward the ground.

"Honey?"

It was Mama. Her room opens through big glass-paned doors onto the porch, just like mine. She was standing in the doorway, the lace curtains bil-lowing around her. "Honey, you planning to stay out there and let it rain all over you?"

"I'm just watching it roll in, Mama."

"Well, it's *here*. Come on in now, quick."

She switched on a lamp, and her room glowed through the doorway. The pink rosebuds in her wallpaper looked ready to bloom. I walked across the damp porch and pushed through the door curtains. I sat down on a footstool. Leaning back, I lay my head against the bed and looked up at the ceiling. There were dark stains on it. "Does the roof still leak in here, Mama?"

"It sure does." She settled into the big flowered chair by the lamp. "That's why I keep that pail by the wall. I feel like Noah's wife every time it rains."

I rocked back and forth on the footstool. "I don't mind the rain much."

"At least it cools things off a little bit. Lord knows we need that. I think it's the war that's making things hot. All those bombs and planes affecting the stratosphere or whatever it is."

"I don't think it's the war, Mama. I think it's just Nature."

"Don't ask me. I just know it's so hot I've been keeping my nylon stockings in the refrigerator. That way they're cool to wear, and Aunt Roselle says they last better. I hope she's right. They're my last pair, and when they go I'm done for." She fanned her throat with her hand. "Course it used to get hot before the war too. That time I was Queen of the Apple Parade I almost fainted from the heat. And it was hot at those dances Pat and I used to go to. It was in the nineties at the one where we met."

"You met Daddy at a dance?"

"Didn't I ever tell you that? Well, I did, at one over in Asheville, right after I graduated from high school. He walked up with that red hair of his all slicked back and broke in on me. Before the evening was over, he broke in fourteen more times. Total of fifteen! He told me he just couldn't resist my 'sky-blue eyes.' "

"What did people say?"

"It was a scandal. He ended up in a fistfight with the boy who brought me. And was I furious! Told him I never wanted to lay eyes on him again, sky-blue ones or not. But the next day he came by the house with some flowers he'd picked—and one of *his* eyes was black. He looked so sweet and sheepish I just had to let him in. Six months later we were *married.*"

"Daddy had a black eye?"

"Lord, yes. And that wasn't the last one he got. He was real rambunctious back then." She pushed a finger at my knee. "Listen to this: One night not long after we were married we went to a square dance down by Saluda Lake, and this man on the sidelines kept whistling at me every time we'd promenade past. Well, after about three times Pat just said, ''Scuse me, Bess, honey,' walked over, picked up that man, and threw him in the lake!"

I pounded my fist on the bed. "Daddy just picked him up?"

"Big man too! Just picked him up and threw him in the *water*. Course we had to leave right away, that very minute—the man was related to half of Saluda. But we didn't stop laughing till we got back to Pinehill. Oh, Law, we used to have fun." She smiled, but in a way that looked more sad than happy. "Pat was so wonderful. Always here when I needed him. Always so sweet. He was—" She touched her lips. "Pat was—"

I thought she was going to cry. I got up and put my arm around her. "Mama, he's all right. He's gonna come home all right."

"Of *course* he's all right," she said, straightening up. "It's just this heat that's getting me down. And then the rain, and then the heat worse than before." She turned away from me. "And no parties and no dances—and never any fun." She picked up her hand mirror from the dressing table and looked hard at herself.

Now, Mama is really pretty; everybody in Pinehill says so. She has brown hair that's wavy and turns up around her cheeks. Sometimes the waves shine like gold. Her eyes are sky blue, just like Daddy said. She likes to laugh. I can't imagine anybody prettier, but she said, "I look just awful. All this worrying and frowning is doing it." She found a powder puff and patted her face. "What *will* I look like when Pat comes home?"

I started to tell her she'd look just fine, but she said, "I did get one compliment today. Henry Cawley said I was still the prettiest Pinehillian he'd ever seen, or something to that effect. I know he was just being a gentleman, but it did me good to hear it." She turned her head from side to side in front of the mirror. "He even wanted me to go for a joyride in his new car. Lord knows I wanted to, but I said no, people might talk. Still, it's such a pretty new car. . . ."

The idea of my mother riding around the mountains with anybody not my father was so shocking to me I couldn't even picture it. "I don't like Tal anymore," I said.

"But, Son, he's your best friend."

"He was, but he's not anymore." I went to the door and scowled out at the rain. "He thinks he knows everything."

"He gets that from his father," she said, laughing. "His father acts like he invented electricity."

"I wish *my* father was here. There's a lot of stuff I need to talk to him about."

"Why, honey, anything you want to say to Daddy you can say to me too."

"Oh, Mama . . . I don't think—" I could feel my cheeks getting red.

"Yes, sir, you come right over here and tell me what it is."

"But—"

"Come on now."

I walked back to Mama's chair and sat down in front of her. "Well, see . . . okay, see, I've been wondering about some things. I've been wondering about when a man—"

"Yes, honey?" She put her hand on my shoulder.

"Well, when a man and a woman . . . you know . . . want to start a baby?"

Mama's fingers tightened. She looked for a second like a rabbit who's just discovered a trap around it. Flicking her eyes over the room, she glanced up at the ceiling. "Lord, look!" she said, relieved. "It's starting to leak. Grab that pail!"

"What . . . ?"

"Quick, child! Before we're washed away!"

I saw water forming on the plaster overhead. I grabbed the tin pail from the corner and shoved it onto the bed under the leak.

"Oh!" she said, slapping her hand against her chest. "I don't know *what* I would've done without you." The drops splattered. She babbled on about the leak, about how I'd come to her rescue.

I guess I babbled some too.

☆   ☆

Mama and I talked about a lot of things at supper that night, but not about what I'd asked her. It was okay. I'd ask Charlie about it tomorrow.

I went up to my room early. I got in bed and took out the Ernie Pyle dispatch on D-Day that Aunt Roselle had sent me. Ernie is the most famous reporter of the war. He's already covered the battles in North Africa, and now he's going along with our men in Europe. He always stays beside the soldiers on the front lines. They all know about him and they love him because he's one of them. He's my favorite writer.

As I read Ernie's description of the invasion, I pictured myself right there in the landing boat with Daddy. I saw us moving up to the beach with shells slamming overhead, mines exploding in the water. I could feel the boat ram into the sand, see the front fall open for us to jump out. The water would be cold and choppy when we hit it, maybe over my head, but Daddy would grab the back of my collar and pull me to shore. The enemy gunfire would be so heavy we'd be pinned down on the beach. Exploding shells would throw sand and stones over us. The big guns on the ships would finally give us cover. Crouching low, spraying bullets, we'd run for the high ground together. . . .

The last of Ernie's dispatch told how the shoreline looked after the battle had been won. The wreckage was terrible—knocked-out tanks, burned jeeps, big derricks twisted out of shape. "But there was another and more human litter," he wrote. "It extended in a thin little line, just like a high-water mark, for miles along the beach. This was the strewn personal gear, gear that would never be needed again by those who fought and died to give us our entrance into Europe.

"There in a jumbled row for mile on mile were soldiers' packs. There were socks and shoe polish, sewing kits, diaries, Bibles, hand grenades. There were the latest letters from home, with the address on each one neatly razored out—one of the security precautions enforced before the boys embarked.

"There were toothbrushes and razors, and snapshots of families back home staring up at you from the sand. There were pocketbooks, metal mirrors, extra trousers, and bloody, abandoned shoes. There were broken-handled shovels, and portable radios smashed almost beyond recognition, and mine detectors twisted and ruined."

As Ernie walked along the sand, he saw a dog up ahead. The dog must have come ashore with some of our soldiers and lost them during the battle. "He stayed at the water's edge," wrote Ernie, "near a boat that lay twisted and half sunk at the waterline. He barked appealingly to every soldier who approached, trotted eagerly along with him for a few feet, and then, sensing himself unwanted in all the haste, he would run back to wait in vain for his own people at his own empty boat."

Ernie stepped over the body of a soldier who he thought was dead. But when he looked down, he saw that the soldier was only sleeping. "He lay on one elbow," Ernie said, "his hand suspended in the air about six inches from the ground. And in the palm of his hand he held a large, smooth rock.

"I stood and looked at him a long time. He

seemed in his sleep to hold that rock lovingly, as though it were his last link with a vanishing world. I have no idea at all why he went to sleep with the rock in his hand, or what kept him from dropping it once he was asleep. It was just one of those little things without explanation that a person remembers for a long time."

I wondered if that could be Daddy lying there, holding on to that stone. If it was, would Ernie stop and be his friend? And that poor little dog, running up and down the beach, looking for someone.

It's the same with Mr. Whitmire, I thought. Alone and tired and sad. Nobody to take care of you.

I'll take care of you.

YOU JUS' ATE BREAKFAST, Mr. Cam. What you needin' mo' food for?"

"To take with me hiking, Lyda. I'm staying out all day."

"Clean till suppertime?"

"Sure. Now, just some iced tea and some ham biscuits. And three of those hard-boiled eggs, and some celery, and two pieces of cake. And a hambone."

"A *bone.*"

55

"You're such a good cook, Lyda, I can't stop eating. Bones and all."

"Mr. Cam, I don't know what's goin' on, but long's you got a good appetite I s'pose it don't matter." She took the army pack I handed her and began to fill it with food. "Don't you eat all this at one sittin'," she told me, "you hear?"

"Thanks, Lyda. I won't." I hitched the pack onto my shoulders and went out the back door. I could get to Mr. Whitmire's cabin by crossing the orchard and going through the woods, but I wanted to go past Charlie Cogswell's store.

Charlie's store was one of the first buildings put up in Pinehill. It stands right beside the main road, just far enough back for a car to pull up in front. It's made out of wood, painted white, and it has a tin roof. There's a porch on the front and another one above that, outside the rooms where Charlie lives. When the war started, he bolted a flagpole to the upper railing. Every day now from sunup till sunset he keeps an American flag flying from it.

There are two big glass windows at the front of the store. As I came up, I could see Charlie working inside at the counter. No one else was around. I opened the screen door and said, "Hey."

"Hey, son," he said, waving me in. "How you doing?"

"Fine."

"I am too. I'm putting together a list of the battles our Pinehill boys have fought in." He brushed off a sheet of paper, careful not to smear it. "See, here's Ed Allen. He was at Palermo and Monte Casino. Here's Joe Mack Johnson, Guadalcanal . . . and look here, boy, here's Pat."

After Daddy's name was printed "D-Day." "Gosh, Charlie, that's the biggest one of all."

"It is, it sure is. I'm so proud of Pat I could bust." He took the list and tacked it on the wall next to the war map. "Now what I need is a snapshot of each of the boys to go along with their battles. Showing their uniforms and all."

"I can get you one of Daddy."

"Can you?"

"Sure. He sent me some from England. He's standing in front of a castle over there."

"That's just exactly what I need." He pulled at the skin on his neck. "In fact, do you think you could get me two of 'em?"

"Well, I guess so. But how come?"

Charlie leaned low against the counter and dropped his voice to a whisper. "I haven't told anybody yet, Cam, but I'm getting an emergency outpost ready up in the mountains. I want duplicates of all my war records to keep inside it."

The hairs along the back of my neck pricked up. "What for, Charlie?"

"I'll tell you what for. You remember those two German submarines that landed a while back? In

57

Florida and up in New York State? When those Nazi spies came ashore?" I nodded, and he narrowed his eyes. "Well, what do you think is halfway between those two spots?"

"Washington, D.C.?" I whispered.

Charlie stood up and looked peeved. "Pinehill, North Carolina!" he said. "Right *here.*"

"But, Charlie—"

"But nothing. I figure those spies, if they hadn't got caught, were gonna converge on this area and set up a hideout. For a *very* important person."

"You mean for . . . ?"

"For *Adolf Hitler,* that's who I mean. For when he loses the war. They've tried to do it once; mark my words, they'll try again."

My stomach turned over. "But, Charlie," I said, "why would Hitler come *here?*"

"Because nobody'd ever think of looking here, that's one reason. And those mountains up there are just like Germany, that's one more. And there's a *third* reason."

"There is . . . ?"

Charlie leaned down again. His hair had stayed combed as long as it could, and it flopped recklessly out over one ear. "Only a few people know this, Cam, what I'm 'bout to tell you. Are you ready?"

"I—I think so."

"To begin with, you know all about the tower over at the Cawley Home, don't you? The millionaire, the screaming wife, the crazy people?"

"And the skeletons?"

"That's right. Well, it was closed up for years, back in the 1920s. Not a soul lived there except for one man—this strange-looking caretaker with mad-looking eyes. He almost never said a word, but when he did he had this rumbling foreign accent."

"I never heard about him before," I said.

"Well, not many people remember him nowadays. But back then everybody was real suspicious of him. I mean he was *peculiar*. He kept a candle burning up in that tower all night long."

"Up there with all those skeletons?"

"Peculiar as all get-out. One night my cousin Wilson snuck into the building to find out what he was up to. He got in through a window and found the staircase that leads up the tower. It's a big spiral one. Sure enough, candlelight was coming from under the door high up at the top. Wilson climbed the steps one by one, not making a sound. He got to the end and eased open the door."

My hairline was tingling. "Did he see the skeletons?"

"He saw the skeletons all right. But that wasn't the worst. In the middle of the room, sitting at a table, was that strange foreign man. He was dressed all in black. There was a globe of the world beside him, and he was writing on page after page of old yellowed paper. Slowly, like he'd been waiting for him, he looked up at Wilson with those mad eyes of his, eyes that burned right through my poor cousin.

Like two white-hot knives cutting through flesh. Like Knives of Death."

"Is th-that when Wilson lost the feeling in his hands?"

"*And* his hair turned white. He fainted dead away, and the next thing he knew he was lying on the grass outside the tower, and it was dawn."

"And he couldn't feel a thing?"

"And white-headed to boot. He came straight here and told me it was the worst night of his life. And here's the P.S.: Nobody ever saw that caretaker again. He left North Carolina that very night."

I let the story sink in. I'd heard plenty about the tower, but this was the worst part of all. "But, Charlie," I said, "what does that have to do with Adolf Hitler?"

"That *was* Adolf Hitler."

"What?"

"Absolutely. Wilson and I didn't figure it out till years later. We saw a picture in *Life* magazine of this man who was leading what they called the Nazi party over in Germany. He had black hair brushed at an angle across his forehead. He had this square mustache. He had these crazy eyes."

"It was the caretaker?"

"The *very* same. And we understood then what he'd been writing every night in the tower. He'd been working on that evil book of his, *Mein Kampf,* and planning how to take over Germany. And finally the world."

"A-and you think he might come back?"

"I'm sure of it. He was safe here once, and he thinks he can be again. Yep, sooner or later this place is gonna be crawling with Nazis. That's when I'm heading for my outpost in the mountains. I can hold out indefinitely up there."

Oh, Lord, I thought, the enemy right here in Pinehill. I could feel the war moving in on me, all around me. Sometimes I wanted to be part of it, but right now the whole thing just scared me to death.

The bell over the front door jangled, and I jumped halfway across the store. A man was standing in the doorway, dark against the light outside. I saw that it was Mr. Cawley, and I let my breath out. I was glad to see anybody who wasn't wearing a swastika.

"Charlie, my boy," he said, walking up to the counter, "get me out your best watermelon. Gonna take it down by a stream and have a picnic." The bell jingled again, and he looked back like he was expecting somebody. Mama walked in.

Mama was with Henry Cawley.

"Oh, hey, Son," she said, all breathless. "I didn't see you. It's so dark in here after being out in that sun." She had on high-heeled yellow shoes. She joined Mr. Cawley at the counter. "Hey to you, too, Charlie."

Charlie looked as surprised as I was to see them, but he tried to be nice. "Good morning to you, Bess."

"We want us a watermelon," said Mr. Cawley

again. Mama laughed and swatted him on the arm. "You really serious about a picnic, Henry?"

"Course I'm serious. Everybody knows I'm a serious man. Ain't that right, Charlie?"

"You're serious, all right."

"See there, Bess? Now, Charlie, pick us out a good one."

Mama came over and ruffled my hair with her fingers. All she said was, "Henry's car is so fancy inside. It's a 1942."

"The last car out of Detroit," said Cawley, "before they stopped making 'em. Told the government I had to have it for the old folks up at the Home." He and Mama both laughed.

"This one oughta be just fine," said Charlie, holding up a long green melon.

"Put it on the Home bill," said Cawley, "and lay it in the back of my Packard. On the floor, not on the upholstery." He took Mama by the arm and followed Charlie to the door. "By the by, Charlie," he said, "when you gonna get rid of your old jalopy? I bet it hardly makes it to Hendersonville."

Charlie turned back to him. In spite of the melon on his shoulder, he straightened up tall. "Not till the war is over," he said, looking for all the world like a five-star general, "and every one of our Pinehill boys is back home."

Cawley tried to keep from guffawing, but not very hard. "Well, that's mighty patriotic of you," he said.

As Charlie went out the door, Mama looked back at me. "You coming with us, Cam?"

"Um . . . no, ma'am. I'm gonna stay here a while."

"You not planning to ask Charlie any *questions*, are you?" She gave a little smile and looked at Henry Cawley. "He's getting to *that* age, you know."

Mama! Don't tell him.

"What age is that?" said Cawley.

"Oh, you know—getting interested in what he ought not to."

"You a little young for that, ain't you?" Cawley said. He scowled down at me. "My boy Talbert's older'n you and he's not letting that kind of thing come near to crossing his mind."

"Tal's my boy's best friend," said Mama.

"No, he's *not*," I said. "Not anymore."

"Well, I for one am glad of that," said Cawley. "I don't want any boy with thoughts like yours hanging 'round my Talbert."

"Oh, Henry, don't be so stuffy." Mama smiled again and patted my shoulder. "We're just teasing you, Cam." She went out the door with Cawley. Her yellow shoes were bright in the sun. She glanced back at me for a second, just a quick look before she got in the car.

As soon as they drove off, I picked up my pack and slipped out the side door of the store. I couldn't face Charlie.

I CUT ACROSS THE FIELD behind the store. Not looking back, I hurried up into the woods. I was glad to be hidden by the trees.

I scuffed my shoes into the topsoil, cutting through to red clay. It glistened, slick and new as Cawley's car. Cawley! I could see him sitting with Mama out by a creek somewhere. He'd be spitting watermelon seeds over his shoulder, pleased with himself. Mama would be more delicate—she'd be cutting a little square of melon and raking off the seeds, slipping it into her mouth. She'd be chatting and laughing about how this summer is almost as hot as that time she was Queen of the Apple Parade. He'd be saying, "My, and you're still just as pretty as you were then."

Damn!

If he's such a ladies' man, I thought, how come he's not married? His wife died years ago, when Tal was a baby, and he's been alone ever since. Miss Airie Mitchell at the post office is always saying what a fine man he is and how we ought to feel sorry for him. I think she's sweet on him. Fine, let her have him! But today I didn't feel sorry for him at all!

I climbed the path to the top of the hill, to where the trees ended and grass started on the other side. I could see a stone dam down below, with Davis Pond beside it. Past the water the land sloped up toward the forest where Mr. Whitmire was hidden.

I walked down to the edge of the pond. It was dark to look into, like a flat black mirror. Kneeling down, I could see myself with clouds around me. Everything was upside down. I turned my head to try to right the reflection, but as I did I caught a funny movement in the reeds that grew on the other side of the pond. They eased apart, and a dark muzzle poked through.

I ducked lower—she was still the meanest-looking dog I'd ever seen—and watched her lap up the water. She did it fast, like she hadn't had any in a long time. After she finished, she climbed out of the reeds and trotted off, not up toward the cabin, but off through a low place between the hills.

I picked up my pack and ran across the top of the dam to the far side of the pond. With her gone, meeting Mr. Whitmire would be a lot easier. Of course he wouldn't know who I was. But I'd just say, "I'm Campbell Reed, Mr. Whitmire. My great-aunt is Eulalee Bethune, who knows you." And I'd show him the ham biscuits I brought. And I'd tell him he didn't ever have to go back to the Cawley Home. "I'll take care of you, Mr. Whitmire," I'd say. "Don't you worry."

I climbed the hill to where the woods started and pushed in along a path. This way was a lot simpler than coming from the opposite direction, along Dead End Trail. In only a couple of minutes I could see the cabin through the trees. It looked like no one had come near it in years—boarded windows, door hanging open, nothing but blackness and silence inside. Mr. Whitmire was nowhere in sight. I stopped at the edge of the clearing, hoping he'd see me and come out from wherever he was. "Mr. Whitmire?" I called, not very loud. "Mr. Whitmire, I'm Campbell Reed . . ."

Well, maybe he's asleep, I thought. He's so old maybe he's just lying inside taking a nap. Or maybe—and this was a terrible notion—maybe he's *dead.*

All of a sudden I wanted to get as far from that cabin as I could. I'd never seen a dead person before, and I didn't want to start now, not all alone in a pitch-black cabin. I turned around to go straight home, but I didn't get to take a single step: the dog was back. She was standing on the path in front of me, a dead squirrel in her mouth. Just as surprised as I was, she dropped the squirrel. In a fury, she rushed me.

All I could do was throw myself toward the cabin. The pack flew out of my hands and scattered biscuits across the clearing. I scrambled up the steps, fell through the door into the darkness, slammed it behind me. A half-second later she lunged against it, tearing at it with nails and teeth.

I pressed my back to the wood and tried to hold it shut. It banged like crazy every time she hit it. I felt an old wooden table at my side, and I dragged it over to block her as long as I could. Blind, shaking, I let go and stumbled farther into the dark of the cabin. I felt my way along the walls, rough wood that had never been plastered. Bird feathers were caught in the crevices, pine needles, brittle twigs. . . .

My hand came to something clammy. I snatched it back, but bony fingers touched my shoulder. Dead people and skeletons and Nazis went skittering through my head. I jerked away—but that bony hand gave me a little pat. It was like a leaf settling on my shoulder.

"Mr. Whitmire?" I whispered. "You ain't dead?"

☆   ☆

I sat on the edge of the porch with my back against one of the posts. Below me on the ground lay the dog. She was concentrating on the bone I'd brought her. Even so, she kept one eye cocked on me. I didn't look back at her. If you stare a strange dog in the eye, it thinks you're making a challenge. I sure didn't want any more of that.

Mr. Whitmire sat on the porch a few feet away from me. I'd salvaged some of the ham biscuits for him. He'd eaten them and drunk the tea, but he hadn't acted hungry at all. He'd just chewed and swallowed like he didn't even know he was doing it. He hadn't said a word. Cawley was right about that—his mind was just rotted away.

He might've looked good once, but he was terrible-looking now. The only hair he had left stuck out like sweaty feathers along the sides of his head. He had a thousand wrinkles. The deepest ones started up at the corners of his eyes and ran all the way down his cheeks. They were like gutters for his eyes to dribble into. His neck was all gutters too—no, more like a collection of strings that branched out into his shoulders and then on out into his arms and long skinny fingers. All he had on was a pair of beat-up shoes, some torn trousers, and an old stained undershirt, the kind with no sleeves. It was so thin and loose you could see the bent-in bones in his chest. And he was sunburned. It probably hurt, but he didn't seem to know it.

The three of us just sat there. Since I was the only one who knew how to talk, it got to be pretty quiet. Finally, to keep myself awake, I got a sheet of paper out of my pack and wrote a letter to France.

In the letter I told Dad how proud everybody was of him for being in D-Day. I said when I grew up I wanted to be a hero like he was, landing on beaches, blowing up tanks. I made him promise not to tell, and then I told him about Mr. Whitmire and how I was hiding him. "I'm sitting with him this very minute," I wrote. "He would probably send a hello to you, but he's so old he forgot how to talk." I told him I hoped he hurried home because I had something to ask him. I said I loved him and missed him very much. I didn't mention Mama.

I finished the letter and slid it into my pack. "Well, Mr. Whitmire," I said, "I just wrote a letter to my dad. That's what I was just doing, with that pencil." He didn't turn his head. "Yep," I said louder, "my dad's in the army over in France. He was in on D-Day."

Nothing.

Not even a blink. Only the dog looked up and frowned, like I was disturbing her concentration.

This is dumb, I said to myself. Here I am baby-sitting a crazy old man and a mean old dog. I bring lunch, I try to be nice. And what for? One doesn't even know I'm here; the other one wants to bite me.

I got up to leave. The dog scrambled to her feet to warn me that she was on guard, but I didn't pay any attention. "Mr. Whitmire," I said, "I got to be going." Of course he didn't even look around. "Well, good-bye," I said.

Just when I was ready to walk off, he swiveled slowly around. He held out his finger toward me. For a second I thought he was pointing at something. He wiggled it, and I realized he wanted me to take hold of it. Thinking how crazy it was, I wrapped one hand around it. When I did, he pulled back and let out this burp you could've heard all over Pinehill. It was the first sound he'd made for me. I pulled on his finger again to make sure: *buurrp!*

I dropped his hand and started to laugh. Thanks for the ham biscuits, he was saying. Enjoyed 'em, come back soon, you hear?

ENRY, YOU ARE *SO* sweet to take us riding on a hot day like this." Mama turned the window so air would rush back against her face. She glanced over her shoulder at me in the back seat. "Is that too much breeze on you, Cam?"

Pouting as hard as I could, I didn't answer. This little trip wasn't *my* idea—riding with Mr. Cawley and Tal to Asheville for lunch. Mama thought it up and made me come along. I didn't tell her how I felt about it. It was bad enough when they rode around alone, but making me part of it . . . well, I just didn't have words for it.

Tal wasn't happy either. He didn't care about his father being out with my mother, he just hated being stuck in the back seat with the Spitwad. We rode along not saying a word. He sulked out his window, I sulked out mine.

At least I'd gotten to visit Mr. Whitmire again before we left. I went first thing in the morning with another day's supply of food. He burped and the dog growled, and that was it.

"I declare," said Mama, "riding around is the only cure for this hot weather."

"That's why I got my new car," Cawley said. "I could tell the climate was changing—getting hotter every year. No doubt 'cause of the war and all."

"I agree."

"All them bombs and planes. So I bought me my Packard to cool off in."

"Course you still have to watch out for your gas," said Mama, sighing. "There's always something to spoil things."

"Oh, I got plenty of ration coupons, Bess, don't you worry." He winked at her. "I convinced the government I oughta get unlimited gas because of the Home: 'automobile used in the line of work.'"

"You're so lucky, Henry. Eula's only allowed three gallons a week. Three! It's terrible."

Cawley grinned and said he had a way around

everything. "If you're real smart, you can even profit from these shortages—get hold of something other people want, and then charge whatever you please for it."

"But who's got anything to sell?"

"You'd be surprised, Bess." He glanced in the rearview mirror to make sure Tal and I weren't paying any attention. "Open the glove compartment," he said quietly. He put his finger to his lips.

I heard the catch click open. Mother gave a little gasp. "Henry," she whispered, "a pair of *nylons.*"

"And that's just the tip of the iceberg."

"But where did you *get* them? I can't find a pair anywhere."

"The government's using all available nylon for parachutes, Bess. Only a very few factories are still allowed to produce stockings. And *one* of them—" he chuckled low—"belongs to Jeddah Whitmire's late daughter's husband."

"You mean—?"

"Precisely," he whispered. "Instead of paying old Jeddah's bill in dollars, he pays in nylon stockings. Which I sell to a man in Charlotte for three times the cost of Jeddah's keep."

"Henry, how enterprising!"

"That is the very word for it. Made me enough money already for the down payment on this car."

"But, Henry," whispered Mama, "with Mr. Whitmire gone—"

Cawley kept his voice low, but there was a mean

sound to it now. "You have hit the nail on the head. With that old so-and-so gone, my stocking supply is flat terminated. I could strangle him, if he wasn't already lying out somewhere dead as a raccoon!"

"Now, Henry."

He cleared his throat. "You're right," he said. "We are all facing bad times these days, and we must be lenient. To show I'm not such a bad man, I want you to have that pair of nylons. Yes, I do."

"Oh, Henry!"

"Don't worry, I still got a fair supply left."

"Oh, *thank you*," she whispered. "My last pair is in shreds! Why, I'd slip these on right now if I weren't such a lady."

That did it.

I heaved myself up so my face was right beside Cawley's head and shouted, *"I heard every word you said!"*

"What—!"

"President Roosevelt says men like you are hurting the war effort! He calls 'em *black marketeers!*"

Cawley almost lost control of the car. Tal shouted, "You take that *back!*"

"I won't neither!" I hollered. *"Hurting the war effort!"*

Tal hauled off to whack me, but Mama's arms shot in between us. "Now listen, *both* of you!" She was hanging over the front seat, holding us apart. "We are out for a *nice time*. There aren't many nice times

74

these days, so don't spoil it." She looked hard at us, especially me. *"Understand?"*

"But—!"

"No buts!"

Cawley got his voice back. "I will tan that boy's—!"

"You *too*, Henry. Not a *word*." She slapped her palm on the back of the seat. Mama can be real firm when she wants to. *"Now,"* she said, seeing we weren't going to burst out again, "let's have us a nice time." She rounded her cheeks in that Apple Queen smile of hers and settled into her seat. She fluffed her skirt. "I just wish I'd worn something *pretty* for the occasion."

Cawley threw one last nasty glance at me. He coughed twice, spit out the window, and said, "You look mighty good to me, Bess."

"Oh, Henry, you're teasing."

"I'm *not* teasing. You're pretty as a picture."

"Now I know you're teasing." She punched his arm with her finger. "All you men are just alike."

I thought I would die if I had to listen to any more. I saw a roadside stand up ahead. "Oh boy," I said, "a store. Let's stop, oh boy."

"Oh, *yes*," said Mama. "They've got some fresh mountain honey. Eula's been wanting some."

"What about Asheville and lunch? We ain't got all that much time."

"Please, Henry, I want some honey."

Sighing, Cawley turned the car off the road and rolled up to the store. It was one of those shacklike places you see all over the mountains. They sell everything imaginable. Concrete flamingos and stone dwarfs and birdbaths were lined up along the edge of the road; bright cotton bedspreads hung on a line behind them.

I jumped out and pretended to be fascinated by one of the Seven Dwarfs. When Mama and Cawley started talking to the woman who ran the place, I slipped out of sight behind the spreads and tried to take a deep breath.

I couldn't believe what was happening. My mother was out gallivanting around the mountains with a black marketeer—and I was her accomplice. What would Daddy say? I was supposed to take care of her, but I was letting him down!

The spread I was behind swelled slowly in the breeze. It was yellow, with little tufts of yarn all over it. The others in the row were pink and white and light green. They looked like big billowy sails. I wanted to tie them together to carry Mama and me away, so we'd never see Cawley again.

A blue spread at the end of the row lifted with air, and I saw Tal standing behind it. His cheeks were wet. With a quick movement he rubbed a corner of the cloth across his eyes.

I thought Talbert Cawley had never cried in his life. Maybe he was wishing he could fly away too.

I walked over to him, but he turned his back. "Tal," I said, "I didn't mean to hurt your feelings." He didn't look at me. "Honest. I don't care what your dad does with those stockings."

He turned around. His eyes had gathered color from the spreads around us. They were darker than I'd ever seen them. His earlobes were red. He reached in the pocket of his shirt and pulled out a single cigarette. He put it between his lips and lit it with a match.

To hide my surprise, I began to study the spread next to us. There was a peacock woven into it. Its tail, open like a fan, was almost as wide as the cloth itself. I ran my finger around the soft outline of its head.

"Look here, boy."

Tal narrowed his eyes and blew a long plume of smoke at me. When the breeze had cleared it away, he held the cigarette right under my nose. "Take a good look," he said.

"I see it."

"That's good. 'Cause one of these days, one day real soon, I'm gonna catch up with you. I'm gonna catch up with you and beat you bloody for what you said about my father. And after I do, I'm gonna take a cigarette, one just like this, and make you smoke it till you puke all over yourself. And run home crying. Puke and blood and snot and tobacco all over you." He gave me a shove. "You hear me, boy?"

I started to walk away, but he caught my arm.

"You like that bird, don't you?" He took another drag on the cigarette. Deliberately, he held it out and burrowed it into the bedspread. He burned a round black hole through the peacock, through the heart.

☆   ☆

I lay awake in my room that night. There was no moon. The porch outside and the yard past that and the mountains even farther on were as dark as if a blackout had been declared across all of North Carolina.

I switched on the table lamp beside my bed. It made a circle of light that fell across my covers and onto the floor. It was weak and flickering, not strong enough even to reach the walls of my room. It semed like the only light left in the world.

I opened a drawer beneath the lamp and got out a new Ernie Pyle clipping that Aunt Roselle had sent me. I pulled the covers up to my neck and started to read.

In this dispatch Ernie told about spending the night after D-Day in an apple orchard, just like the ones here in Pinehill. It was dark when he got to the orchard, so he and the soldier he was with took some rations out of their jeep and began to eat supper. "While we were eating," he wrote, "the first German planes of the night came over. One dropped its bombs not very far away—near enough to give us our first touch of nerves. There were antiaircraft guns all around and they made an awful racket. The night began to take on an ominous and spooky aspect. We felt lonely."

They went to bed with their heads under the jeep for protection, but they couldn't sleep because of the booming of the guns. "Sometimes planes would come in low, and we would lie there scrunched up in knotty tenseness, waiting to be hit."

At dawn they got up. A colonel made a reconnaissance tour of the area they'd slept in. "When he came back," wrote Ernie, "he said that our little orchard, which looked so rural and pretty in the dawn, was full of dead Germans, killed the day before. We would have to help bury them pretty soon. That was our first night in France."

I folded the clipping, put it carefully back in the drawer and snapped off the lamp. It was a long time before daylight came.

I WAS SO GLAD TO GET to the cabin the next morning that I didn't even mind when the dog leaped up and bristled. "Mr. Whitmire," I said, coming up to the porch, "it's me again."

There was shade against the wall of the house, but he was sitting on the top step in the hot sun. He came out of his blank stare enough to squint at me. I was pretty sure he knew who I was. "I brought you this hat," I said. It was a straw one I'd gotten out of Daddy's closet. I had a fresh blue shirt for him too. I took off the hat and held it out to him. "It's good for keeping the sun off." He didn't move, so I reached up and slipped it onto his head.

The wide brim dropped a shadow over his face. It must've eased the burn on his cheeks and cooled the back of his neck. He smiled at me.

"You look *good*," I said, trying not to sound too surprised. The smile filled out his cheeks, smoothed out his forehead. "Mr. Whitmire, you look *good!*"

"Bet . . . your boots. . . ." His voice was rusty and unsure, like an old Victrola. For a second I thought I hadn't really heard it. He spoke again, clearer: "Bet your boots."

I stared at him. I banged him on the shoulder with my hand. "You can talk," I said. "You *can!*"

The dog saw me hit him. She growled and pushed between us. "Wa-a-it, dog," I said, backing away. "I'm not hurting him!"

Mr. Whitmire laid his hand on her neck. She dropped her hackles, but she flicked her eyes up at me to say I'd better not hit him again.

Gingerly, I held out my hand to her, palm up. She sniffed it suspiciously, then pulled off and looked sulky. "Maybe if I knew her name," I said to Mr. Whitmire, "she'd like me better."

He didn't answer. "Don't you call her something?" I said. "I mean, you named your daughter, didn't you? Eula told me you called her Laura Louise or Clara Louise or something like that." I nodded over at the dog. "You want to name her after your daughter? You want to call her Louise?"

He thought about it for a minute. "Bet your boots," he said.

I held out my hand to the dog again. "Look here, Louise." She examined it doubtfully. Becoming nervous, she flicked her eyes away. She seemed ready to run for the woods. "Louise?" I said. She swayed her tail an inch or two and glanced up at me. When she was like that, not mad or chasing me, she looked kind of sweet.

I don't know what did it—maybe she'd never been called something pretty before—but carefully, almost daintily, she parted her jaws and slipped out her tongue and licked my hand.

"You're a fine dog, Louise," I said.

She looked over at Mr. Whitmire and panted. Her eyes glinted. She seemed to be rejoicing inside. She didn't move much, just swayed from side to side. She looked like she'd found a family at last.

I sat down next to Mr. Whitmire. Louise turned in a satisfied circle and lay down at our feet. I leaned against a post and closed my eyes. Cawley, his Packard, Tal, the war—all my worries seemed to drift off across the mountains. Sitting next to my new friend, our dog keeping watch, I felt like no trouble in the world could get to me. . . .

I heard strange music. Drowsy, I opened my eyes. Mr. Whitmire was humming into a harmonica, making long, leisurely sounds. I listened and decided he was playing "You Are My Sunshine."

I didn't care if I was dreaming. I closed my eyes again. I put my head on a soft place in his shoulder and went to sleep.

☆   ☆

Mr. Whitmire didn't speak again that afternoon. When I left to go home, he tipped his harmonica to his hat. Louise, wagging her tail, followed me to the edge of the clearing. "I'll see you tomorrow," I said to her. "You take good care of things around here."

I walked out of the woods and down to Davis Pond. Beside the water I took off my pack to adjust the straps. That's when I saw Tal. He was sitting on a red clay bank a few yards away. Rob Aiken and Jakie McPhee were beside him. They were just his age and he palled around with them. I didn't like them much.

Since they were between me and the dam, I had to walk past them. When I came near, Tal spit in the grass at my feet. "Don't step on it, runt," he said. "Might make you have a baby." He slapped his knee. Jakie and Rob rolled against him, laughing.

"Cut it out," I said.

He got to his feet. "You make me." Rob and Jakie stood up behind him.

I walked on by. "Don't the runt look cute?" said Jakie. "The *spittin'* image of his daddy!"

"I ain't never seen his daddy," said Rob. "You seen him, Tal?"

"Naw," Tal said, sitting down again. "Ain't nobody seen his daddy. I heard he ain't never had no daddy."

"I seen his mama though."

"*Everybody's* seen his mama." They let out ugly whistles.

I turned around. "How much is your daddy charging for stockings now, Tal?"

In a flash he was standing in front of me, his face inches from mine, his hands balled into fists. He looked very big. "You say that again!"

I swallowed hard. "President Roosevelt says—"

Tal slammed his fist into my chest. I went straight down. "That was for my father," he said, "and this is for *me.*" He kicked out at me. I grabbed his leg and hunched up and bit into it as hard as I could. "Owww!" he hollered. He leaped on me, but he was so angry he landed off balance. I shifted to the side and pulled his collar around. I would've rolled on top of him, but Jakie and Rob hustled up and slammed me down on my back.

They grabbed my arms and legs and held me out flat. Tal, squatting now, rocked on his heels. He wiped the dirt from his jaw, then dived in punching. He drove his fist at my head. I jerked to the side and it jammed in my cheek. A tooth cut the inside of my mouth. I tasted blood.

I twisted over onto my stomach. Jakie said, "No, you don't!" He pushed my face into the ground. Squinting into the dirt, I saw the strangest thing: in the jungle of grass in front of my nose an ant colony was at war with another colony. One group was red; the other was black. Some were rushing about; others were locked in little bunches of hate. They hadn't yet realized we were about to roll over and crush whatever it was they were fighting for.

In that moment I knew the war had come to Pinehill. It had made my friends lie in ambush for me. It had stirred up the ants. Like a heat wave, it had given the whole world fever.

I was part of the war at last, but somehow it wasn't glorious. It just hurt, and it bled, and none of it made much sense. It made me feel ashamed.

Still, you have to fight back.

I lashed out my elbow at Jakie. It caught him in the stomach. Madder than ever, they pulled me onto my back. Tal drew back his fist. Squeezing my eyes shut, I braced myself, but the blow never reached me: from out of nowhere another body heaved onto the pile. Tal hollered; Jakie and Rob leaped up. I heard snarling, snuffling—and there was Louise, terrible, lunging back and forth between them. "Yow!" they screamed. They danced over one another to get away from her. Yelling, not daring even to look over their shoulders, they dashed across the dam. They ran up over the hill toward home.

I dropped my head back against the ground. I began to cry. Louise hurried to me. She stuck her muzzle against my nose, swatted my knee with her tail. Whining, she tried to lick my face clean. She looked up and barked, dashed off and barked again. Turning my head after her, I saw Mr. Whitmire up near the woods. His arms were stretched out in front of him. He was coming down the hill toward me.

I tried to sit up, but I was too dizzy. In a minute his arms were around my shoulders. "Bet your boots," he said. "Bet your boots!" Louise moved up against us, licking him, then me.

I was crying hard now. I pushed my head into his chest. My cheeks wet his clean shirt. "Please, Jeddah," I said, not knowing I would say it, "please come home with me."

S WE CAME ACROSS
the back yard of the Arbor, I saw Lyda staring at us
out the kitchen window. From her expression I knew
how we must look: the oldest man, the dirtiest boy,
and the ugliest dog in Pinehill. She disappeared and I
heard her holler for Eula.

I opened the screen door and showed Jeddah
into the kitchen. Louise stayed close beside us looking
fierce one minute, scared to death the next. Eula hur-

ried in from the front of the house. She took a deep breath and said, "Hello, Jeddah. I'm Eulalee Bethune."

He looked at her as if she were miles away. He didn't say anything, but he took off his hat and held it at his side.

"Are you all right, Son?" she said to me. "There's blood in your hair."

"Yes'm. I'm all right now."

"Well, I imagine you got quite a story to tell." She looked around for Lyda, who was watching through the doorway. "Come on in here and fix these men some lemonade. We gonna sit down and have us a talk."

Lyda shook her head. "I ain't comin' in long's that *wolf's* in there."

Louise started to show her fangs, then wiggled instead. "She won't hurt anybody," I said.

"I know she won't," said Eula, "but put her outside for a while anyway. Here, give her this."

She handed me a hambone. I opened the screen and held it out to Louise. *"Now,* Son," said Eula, sitting down at the table, "tell me what happened."

It came pouring out then, no secret anymore—finding Jeddah, bringing him food, the fight. "And they hit you?" she said.

"Yes'm, but Louise chased 'em off. And Jeddah came and got me. He came all the way down the hill to help me."

She reached across the table and pressed Jeddah's arm. "That was good of you, old friend. Your heart hasn't changed a bit." To me she said, "What do you plan to do now, Son?"

"I'd like Jeddah to live here with us."

"*Here?*" She was full of astonishment. "Lord, child, he's got to go back to Cawley's."

"But, Eula, we've got lots of extra bedrooms. And I'll take care of him, I promise. And he hates it so much at Cawley's. You said yourself it drained all the juice from his life."

"Yes, but—his only relative says he *has* to stay there."

"But he don't *want* to." I turned to Jeddah. "Wouldn't you like to stay here with us, Jed? With me?" I shook his arm. "Huh? In this house? Wouldn't you?"

Slowly the skin around his eyes crinkled. "Bet your boots," he said.

"*There.* See? He wants to stay."

Eula stared at me, then at Jeddah. Shaking her head, she said, "Son, I don't see how he can. He needs—"

Louise growled from the back steps—ugly, surprised, mean. I heard voices from the front hall: Mama was coming in the house and Henry Cawley was with her. Before any of us could move, the kitchen door swung open and they walked in.

Mama stopped short. Cawley, right behind,

bumped into her. He said, " 'Scuse me, Bess" and "Howdy, Mrs. Bethune" before he saw Jeddah. "Great Jumping Jehoshaphat! *Jeddah Whitmire!*"

"Now listen, Henry . . ." said Eula, getting to her feet.

"Jeddah Whitmire!" he said again. *"Alive."*

"Henry, Cam found him up in—"

"Alive!" He was totally dumbfounded. "Not dead in the least!"

"Where *was* he?" said Mama.

Cawley pulled himself together. Not waiting for an answer, he took over like he'd been head of the rescue party. "We may never know all the facts," he said. He came up and wagged his finger at Jeddah. "Course I should be furious at you, yes, I should. Putting me through all that worry and expense. But, no, we just gonna forget all about that now. We just gonna start out new, praising God I finally found you." He looked back at Mama. "As you know, Bess, I was worried sick. In these hard financial times even a single resident is a loss. Especially *this* one." He put his face up to Jeddah's like he was talking to a child, a deaf one, and said, "You're going *home*. Now what do you say to that? Ain't that fine?"

When he didn't get a word back, not even a look, he stood up and said, "Still rotted. Don't know a thing." He ran his fingers along the bones in Jeddah's shoulders. "Ain't in bad physical shape, though. Soon's I get him back to the Home, he'll be fit as ever."

"No," I said. "He ain't going back."

"What's that, boy?"

"He ain't going back. He's staying here with us."

Cawley's face darkened. "Mrs. Bethune, are you aware of this?"

Eula hesitated only a second. "Yes, Henry, I am ... and Cam's right."

"Eula," whispered Mama, "he doesn't belong here with us."

"I should think *not*," said Cawley. "The law says he belongs at the Home."

Eula looked him straight in the eye. "Then show me the commitment papers, Henry."

"Commitment papers—*what* commitment papers? Clara Louise's husband up in New Jersey told me to keep him in the Cawley Home the rest of his life, and he's paying me well to do it. They call that a *verbal* commitment. I don't *need* nothing else!"

He reached out for Jeddah, but I pushed in front of him and shouted, *"You just want nylons for the black market!"*

"What?" said Eula. "Cam, what are you raving about?"

"It's *true!* He gets stockings for Jed's keep and then he sells—"

Cawley shouted me down. "I will *sue* anybody who says any such thing." His face was almost purple. "There's not a lick of proof against me! And anyway it's all perfectly *legal!*"

Eulalee put her hands on her hips. "I should

hope it is, Henry Cawley." She towered as high as she could. "And since you are so well informed about the law, you no doubt know that you need papers from the courts to keep a person in an institution against his will. Mr. Whitmire is a guest in this house, and until you get those papers, he's *staying.*"

"But, Eula," hissed Mama, "he needs keepers. Just look at that shirt."

"That's *Daddy's* shirt," I said, "and it's fresh clean this morning."

"Pat's shirt?" Mama looked at me and saw the blood in my hair. "Son!" she cried, leaning down and holding my shoulders. "Oh, are you all right?"

I struggled away from her. "I'm okay. It's stopped bleeding."

"Talbert Cawley and some older boys waylaid him," said Eula. "If it wasn't for Jeddah he'd be worse off than he is."

"Henry," said Mama, looking up at him, "why would your boy . . . ?"

Cawley made a snorting sound. "You got more sense than to believe *that* story." Backing away from us, he said, "I see you are against me at every turn, Mrs. Bethune. And since you want the very popular Mr. Jeddah Whitmire so bad, you can *have* him." He pushed open the swinging door. "At least till I get the papers. Every kind of papers there is. Then he's going back where he belongs—to *stay.*"

After we heard Cawley's car roar off down the

drive, Eulalee put both hands square on the table. "Well!" she said. "Looks like we got a new member of the household." She held out her hand to Jeddah. Earnestly, he shook it.

"Of course I welcome Mr. Whitmire too," said Mama. "But I don't think it was any of our business to begin with. And I certainly don't like the way you all treated poor Henry." She went out the door, swishing it behind her.

"Poor Henry!" I said.

Eula poked my arm. "Hush, Cam. We got more important things to think about. We gotta put some food in Jeddah—Lyda, start those biscuits!—and some fresh clothes on him. And, Lord yes, a *bath*. Cam, that's your responsibility. Take him up and get him settled in that blue room across from yours and draw him a tub. And give that dog some water. Now, everybody *move.*"

☆　　　　　☆

I don't think Eula meant for me to give Louise a bath, too, but I sneaked her upstairs anyway. As I led her and Jeddah down the hall to the bathroom, she raised her hackles and peered into each room we passed like she expected a bear to be living inside.

The bathroom is old and spacious, with a high window that lets in the afternoon sun. It has black and white tiles on the floor and on the walls. The tub, big enough to haul cotton in, stands on claw feet. I took off my shirt and turned on the tap. I told Jeddah to dump his clothes in the hamper at the other end of the room. He seemed doubtful. "Don't worry," I said, "I'll get you some clean ones after your bath."

He was so slow I decided to bathe Louise first. She saw what was about to happen and tried to skitter past me for the door. I backed her into a corner, put my arms around her, and lifted her into the water. Her paws slipped on the bottom and her head went under. She came up with a desperate snort, splattering water wall to wall. Rearing, she hooked her front legs over my shoulders and hung on for dear life. Even though I soaped her and rinsed her as fast as I could, she rolled her eyes like she'd never been through anything so miserable in her whole existence. For a dog who'd survived on her own in the Blue Ridge, that was saying something.

I pulled the plug, then grabbed a towel from the rack and rubbed her down. Her coat felt nice when it was clean. It was still a peculiar brown, but it was fluffy and soft around her neck. I lifted her out and set her on the floor. "There," I said.

She gave a tremendous shake, nose to tail. Bravely, she went back to the tub and peered at the last of the water whirling down the drain. She poked her nose at my stomach and licked me and shook herself again. Bending her head around, she ran her tongue over the fluffy hair on her shoulders.

I laughed and turned to see if Jeddah was watching. He was standing by the clothes hamper, smiling at me. He was naked. Only his straw hat still sat on his head.

I studied him for a minute. Dressed, he'd looked frail, but without clothes he somehow seemed strong and manly. I thought he looked wonderful.

"Will I be like that one day, Jed?"

Before he could answer, I got shy and turned back to the tub. Anyway, I already knew what he would say.

JED'S HERE. . . . MY own friend. . . .

Slowly waking from a dream, I rolled over and opened my eyes. The day was already bright outside. I stretched and felt a strange soreness in my shoulders. My tongue touched a cut inside my mouth. My mind raced back, and I realized that none of it had been a dream. Jed was here!

I threw back the covers and went out to the hall.

I could hear someone playing the old piano down-stairs. I listened hard: a harmonica too!

Still pulling on my clothes, I hurried down to the living room. Eulalee was sitting at the keyboard banging her hands along it like those piano players out West. Jeddah was standing behind her humming busily into his harmonica. I wasn't sure they were playing the same tune—it could've been either "Buf-falo Gals" or "Swanee River"—but when they fin-ished, Eula threw up her hands and said, "That's the best music I ever hope to hear!" She hit another chord. "Jeddah, you know this one? 'Wabash Can-nonball'?"

"Hey," I said.

Jeddah grinned at me. He looked nice in the khaki pants and checkered shirt I'd found for him. "Oh, morning, Son," said Eula. "Well, I haven't played in twenty-five years, and Jeddah's not Harry James—but it *does* sound good. Now, Jeddah, start in right . . . *here.*"

I listened through that one and two more. "Well," I said finally, raising my voice over the music, "I guess I'm gonna go on in and get some breakfast." Nobody paid any attention. "Yeah," I said, "guess I'll just go on in the kitchen and eat me some cereal. You want some, Jed?"

"Lord, Cam!" said Eula. "Can't you see he's *busy?*" She missed a note. "We can't talk now, Son, we gotta *focus.*"

I gave up. I went into the kitchen and sat down at the table. I poured myself some corn flakes. Lyda brought me some milk. "Where's Mama?" I said.

Lyda raised her eyebrows. "Out," she said.

"Out where?"

"Out ridin'. I ain't sayin' with *who*. I'm just sayin' ridin'."

I didn't look up at her. Quickly, I finished my cereal. "Where's Louise?" I said.

"She out workin' on mo' bones. Holler at her."

I got up and opened the screen door. I gave a whistle, and Louise came trotting up. She nuzzled my hand. "Look at that belly," said Lyda. "She gettin' close to time. You oughta be fixin' her a box."

"What kind of box?"

"Box to birth them puppies in. You ain't never seed one? Big box with low sides, full up with newspaper tearin's."

Jeddah came in, stuffing his harmonica in his shirt pocket. Louise barked and wiggled. He folded his arms, ready for whatever we had in mind.

"You know what we oughta do first thing," I said, "is fix Louise up a birthing box. You know? To have her puppies in?"

"Bet your boots," he said.

"Come on." We went out to the garage and found a wooden crate the right size. I piled newspapers into it and we carried them around to the front steps. It was nice there in the early mornings. The little pool in the driveway made it seem cool even when it wasn't. We sat down on either side of the box. I handed Jed half the papers and I took the other half. "Tear off long strips," I said, "and lay 'em in the box. So it'll be soft for the puppies."

Louise poked her nose importantly at the papers. She tried to get in between us, but I made her go down the steps and lie in the drive. "Anyway," I said, "you're getting close to time and you oughta be resting more."

I piled my first batch of strips into the box. I mashed them down to make a firm layer. "You know, Jed, the only thing missing now is the father. There has to've been a father dog. It's just like with people."

Gravely, Jeddah tore a long strip from the front page and then another. I added them to the box. "Who you reckon the father is?" I said. "You reckon it's some other dog that lives in the woods? Maybe he's off somewhere trying to get food for her. Maybe he'll show up any time now."

I fluffed up the second layer of strips. "Tal says in people babies get started with a shot, like a vaccination." I shook my head. "I don't believe a word of it. Do you? I mean, you think babies come from a shot in the bellybutton? Course I know the baby grows in the mother's stomach, but I don't believe it's like Tal says."

Jeddah put down his papers and touched my arm. He looked at me with concentration. He worked his throat. For a minute I thought he was about to say something, but he couldn't seem to form the words. His face clouded over. It was strange; his mind seemed to come and go without any reason. Sighing, he leaned back against the steps.

Below us, Louise stirred and got to her feet. Stretching back from her front legs, she dipped her fat body into a comma. Her haunches and tail lifted high behind her. She reversed herself and strained forward, stretching out one back leg after the other. She followed up with an all-over shimmy. Then she glanced up politely and plodded across the driveway to the pool.

Her movements caught Jeddah's attention. He looked past her at the statue in the water. Pushing the papers away from him, he stood up and went down the steps one by one. He walked to the edge of the pool and squinted at the naked marble girl. After a long time he looked back at me, his eyebrows raised like he knew something special. Sure I was watching, he bent his knees and elbows, mashed his fists tight, and in one short movement bumped his hips forward.

I put down my papers and came over to him. "What is it, Jed?"

Impatiently, he looked at the girl, got ready to bump his hips again, then broke off. His expression cleared. It looked like the sun coming out after a rain. He opened one hand and slowly touched my chest with the end of his fingers. "You ... you're Pat Reed's son."

Ohhh, I *knew* he could talk to me. . . .

I put my hand over his and held it against my shirt. "That's who I am, Jed." I wanted to just stand there with him, but the clearness was already leaving his eyes. Quickly, I pointed at the girl. "You were gonna tell me about—"

It was gone. The vacant look had settled across his face again. "That's all right, Jed." I stroked his hand. "Don't be discouraged." I took his finger and pulled it. He burped, but if you hadn't known it was coming, you'd never have heard it.

"What *are* you all up to?" Eulalee was standing in the front door.

"Just talking," I said, letting Jed's finger drop, "about life."

"Well, *that* should occupy you for a while. But can you leave off for a few minutes?"

"Yes'm."

"Then run to the post office for me, if you will. I'm expecting a package from Roselle today."

"Can Jeddah go?"

"Better not just yet. He's not all that pert. Let him rest while you're gone."

"Okay."

I showed Jed to the hammock that hangs between the pine trees on the other side of the drive. He lay down gladly. I watched him as he went to sleep. A thin tearing from the comic pages was caught on his cuff. His hand slipped from his stomach, and the colored strip fluttered to the grass. I'd seen him when he looked inches from the grave. At that moment, untroubled in his sleep, cartoon characters around him, he seemed years younger than me.

Louise had gone to sleep, too, under the hammock, so I left them and started alone for the post office. It's only a half mile from the Arbor. Except for Charlie's store, it's the only building in Pinehill that people see when they pass through. That's too bad, because it's not like the rest of the town at all. One story, dark green, it looks like a forest ranger's hut. A skinny telephone pole stands beside it. A narrow concrete walk leads from the road to the front door.

Nobody really minds its appearance much except Miss Airie Mitchell, the postmistress, who's famous for being hard to please. Every year she gets up a petition demanding that the postal service tear it down and construct something "more worthy of the Little Charleston of the Mountains." Eula says Miss Mitchell won't be satisfied till the President moves the Washington Monument down here for her to hand out mail in, maybe not even then. Miss Mitchell is forty-two and dyes her hair. She makes it brown, with gold highlights. Eula says she's trying to look like Mama and not coming close.

The door to the post office was open. I went in and saw Miss Mitchell talking over the counter to Mr. and Mrs. Spindale. He's the county magistrate. I know them from church so I said hello, but they were talking so hard, all three of them, they didn't hear me. "Such *bad* judgment," said Miss Mitchell.

"Somebody oughta tell Reverend Healey what she's up to—"

"Taking advantage of a lonely widower," said Mrs. Spindale.

"It's definitely *her* fault," said Mr. Spindale. "With her poor husband in the service and her poor little"—he glanced over at the door and saw me standing there—"*boy,*" he said, nudging his wife with his elbow. She and Miss Mitchell looked around and went white as the envelopes they were holding.

"Why, *Campbell Reed,*" said Miss Mitchell, pulling herself together, "what brings you in today?"

The Spindales started gathering up their mail as fast as they could. "Look how *late* it is!" they said. In two seconds they were out the door.

"Campbell," said Miss Mitchell quickly, "you probably want your mail, don't you? Now, let me see—yes indeed, there's a package from Roselle, and two bills, but nothing from your poor daddy." She clucked her tongue. "Not a thing." She handed me the package and the envelopes. "What is it, something else?"

I looked up at her real hard. "My daddy ain't poor," I said.

She sucked in her breath and put her fingers up to her cheek. She rattled off how she'd never said any such of a thing, never in a thousand years, but I didn't listen. I was already walking out the door.

The Spindales were ahead of me on the concrete walk. Just as they reached the road, Cawley's black

Packard pulled up and Mama got out. She had a daisy in her hair. She shut the door and waved good-bye to Cawley. The Spindales watched him drive off. They glanced at each other, then lifted their heads and marched past Mama without even nodding to her.

She looked surprised, but then she saw me and smiled. She came up and reached out to ruffle my hair. I stepped back. "Stop riding around with Henry Cawley," I said.

"Cam, what . . . ?"

"I said, dammit, you better stop riding all over creation with that damn—with that—" I was starting to cry, I couldn't help it. "With that damn Henry Cawley, or I—I'll—"

Mama looked too shocked even to speak. Out of habit, we turned toward home. We walked a good ten yards, me mumbling and sniffling, before she said, "Cam, please . . . me and Henry aren't doing anything wrong. I promise." She put her hand on my arm. "We're just trying to take our minds off the war. And Pat being over there."

"Don't you blame it on my daddy!"

"No—you don't understand—"

"I don't *have* to understand!" I jerked my arm away. "You ride around in that big shiny car like you—like you're still in the Apple Parade!"

"Cam! Don't say that!"

"You don't care about Daddy!"

"Pat is *all* I care about."

104

"Then *why!*"

The daisy in her hair had slipped from its clip. Her hand fluttered to it and pulled it down. She stared into it. "My birthday was last month," she said quietly. "I wouldn't tell you how old I was . . . remember? That's because I turned thirty. Thirty years old." Her eyes widened, as if she couldn't believe her own words. "When Pat went away, I was only twenty-seven . . . still almost a girl. I couldn't stand it if he came home and I wasn't what he remembered." She pushed the daisy into the pocket of her skirt. "I need someone to tell me I'm still . . . pretty."

"Not Henry Cawley," I said.

"You sound like you're *judging* me."

"The whole town is! That's why the Spindales wouldn't speak to you!"

"What? Why, those old—those *hypocrites!*" She looked angrily back at the post office. Airie Mitchell was watching from the window. "I've got a *right* to have fun if I want to."

"But the war—"

"There's *no war* here in Pinehill!" Her eyes blazed. Her face looked harder than I'd ever seen it. She turned away from me and hurried alone toward home.

☆   ☆

Mama stayed in her room the rest of the day. She didn't come downstairs until suppertime. She passed the corn when Eula asked her, and she nodded when someone spoke, but she never looked at me. And she never once smiled.

I didn't look at her either. I told about building Louise's box, but I told it to Eula. I accidentally dropped a biscuit in the tea, but it was Jeddah I laughed with about it.

After Mama went back upstairs, Eula asked me and Jed if we'd like to sit outside for a while. She turned off the lights and we went out to the front porch. There's a row of big wooden rockers there, and we each took one. A sliver of moon was rising, but there were clouds, and only a little light came through the pines across the drive. Their trunks looked like black bars against the sky. Something howled far off. Louise looked up and sniffed the air. She went nervously to the edge of the porch, then came back and curled up at Jeddah's feet.

"Jed talked a little more today," I said.

"Grand," said Eula. "What did he say?"

"That I was Pat Reed's son."

"He's right about that. You and your papa are about as alike as two people can get."

"Really?"

"Oh yes. When Pat was a boy, he used to spend almost as much time here as he did at his own house. And he was just like you. Smart as a whip most of the time. A daydreamer the rest. A kind, sensitive little boy."

"I'm not sensitive," I said gruffly.

"Well . . . there's nothing wrong with it if you are."

"I know."

She rocked silently for a few minutes. Her head was resting against the back of the chair. "You know something else?" she said finally.

"What?"

"You're a lot like your mother too."

I shifted uncomfortably. "I don't think so."

"Well, you are."

"How?"

"You like to enjoy life, don't you?"

"Yes'm."

"Bess does too. She knows how to have fun, and she shares it. She can come into a room and make every person in it feel happy. People think it's because she's pretty—at a party she looks like something blooming—but it's her spirit that does it."

Looking out at the pines, I tried not to hear her. I felt something building up inside me.

"She's the kind of person I call a 'gift,' Cam. Someone who's put here to make life brighter for the rest of us. But even people like Bess can have failings."

Suddenly I burst out: "Eula, what am I gonna *do?*"

"Shhh, Cam!"

"Daddy left me in charge!"

"Son, Son! That's the hardest lesson in life there is—sometimes there's nothing at all you can do."

IT WAS SUNDAY. I GOT Jeddah dressed in Daddy's blue suit and put on my own suit like it. When we came downstairs, Eulalee was already in the car, grinding the ignition. She had on her Sunday hat. She told me once it's the only hat she ever found that didn't have flowers or feathers or fruit on it. She bought it without even asking how much it was. That was twenty years ago, and she's worn it every Sunday since.

Mama was standing next to the car in her choir

robe. It's wine-colored, with a big white collar. She looked peeved. When we came up, she got inside without saying hello. The car is a gray Chevrolet coupe, with only one seat. Jeddah dipped his hat and crowded in after her.

Louise was sitting in the driveway, heavy and miserable. "We're coming back," I said, patting her head. "It's just church." She rolled her eyes as if she were losing us forever.

Eula flapped her arm out the window. "Hurry up, boy, I almost got it started!" I piled into the narrow space behind the seat. "Let 'er rip," I said.

She pumped her foot and twisted the ignition key again. "You're about to flood it," said Mama.

"Oh, hush up, everybody," Eula said, pumping her foot even faster. "It's hard enough getting this car started without people commenting on everything." The motor made a horrible gagging sound and caught on. "There!" she said. She let out the clutch and we charged off down the drive. I braced myself against the sides of the car. Eula always drives like the wind, and you either hang on or you walk.

"Go *easy*," said Mama, her hands on the dashboard. "I don't want one of my sick headaches up there in that choir."

"I *always* go easy," said Eula. She looked surprised that anyone would think anything else.

"Certainly," said Mama. "At sixty miles an hour!"

We swung onto the main road. Only one brown sedan was up ahead. Eula bore down on it and moved out to pass. The Spindales were inside, all dressed for church. They looked over to nod pleasantly, saw Mama, and hastily turned their faces back to the road. "What's got into *them?*" said Eula.

Mama pressed her lips together. She began to smooth out the folds in her robe. I wanted to reach over the seat and pat her shoulder, but I couldn't bring myself to do it. Instead I said, "What are y'all gonna sing today?"

" 'Have Thine Own Way,' " she said primly. It was almost the first thing she'd said to me in two days.

Eula cleared her throat. " 'Have thine own way, Lord,' " she sang. " 'Have thine own way, Thou art the pot-ter, I am the clay.' " Jeddah felt around for his harmonica, but he'd left it back at the house. He raised his hands and conducted instead. I joined in: " 'Mold me and make me, Af-ter thy will, While I am yield-ed, Wait-ing and still-l. . . .' "

"That's not right," said Mama, irritated. " 'Waiting' comes first. *Then* 'yielded and still.' "

"Why don't you sing it for us, Bess?" said Eula.

Mama turned her head away. "I'm saving my voice for the choir." She looked back in time to see Eula turn off the ignition. "What are you *doing?*"

"Coasting. Good way to save gas."

"Oh, for heaven's sake! Speeding *and* coasting." She reached for her purse. "Where's my aspirin?"

"We're almost there, Mama."

On the left of the road an iron gate hung open between two stone pillars. Eula craned her head out the window, signaled with a big wave of her arm, and swung the car through the entrance. I could see the church up ahead. It sits by itself on top of a rise. It has a steep roof and a three-story bell tower. It was built by Lucius Bethune, the same one who built the Arbor. He had the bricks and stained glass windows shipped over from England. Loti Lowndes, his wife, named it the Church of the Wilderness, because back then this area was as wild as you'd find anywhere.

On the slopes around the church, Lucius had terraces leveled out for a cemetery. All of them are crowded now with stone markers and crosses and tombs. Rusty iron fences divide the plots from each other. In places hemlocks have sprung up and hung their branches out over the terraces. Most of the monuments are carved with Charleston names— Draytons and Middletons and Rutledges. Even Christopher Gustavus Memminger, secretary of the treasury of the Confederacy, is buried here. Some of the tombs are still pretty grand, but one of the oldest is empty. Bootleggers broke into it in the 1920s so they could hide bottles of whiskey inside. It's about three feet high, with a flat stone top and brick sides. People used to drive up secretly and buy liquor from it, just like from a bar.

A path leads through the cemetery to the church. Walking up it between the tombs and the trees and the iron fences is like going through a maze. It's very historical in the daytime, but it's not something you want to do at night. The only creepier place in Pinehill is the tower at the Cawley Home, and this is a close second.

Some ladies in flowered hats were going across to the path when we drove up. They saw Eula coming, and they scattered like hens in front of a tractor. "I'm gonna get that parking place right *there,*" she said, "so Jeddah don't have so far to walk."

"Do just *ease* into it," said Mama.

"Course I will." She steered the car head-on into the space and jammed on the brakes. "Safe and sound!" she said.

Mama flopped the collar of her robe back down and let out her breath. "If I don't end up with a sick headache *this* morning," she said, "I never will." She looked over at Jeddah. "I have to get out for the choir," she said, pronouncing each word carefully. "Do you understand?"

"Mama, he knows that." I reached over his shoulder to open the door. "He knows what he's doing."

Jeddah climbed out and held the door for her. "Thank you very much," she said, each word clear, and hurried up the path.

Eula leaned over and said, "Jeddah, get back in for a minute. And listen to me, Cam. You know we're gonna see Henry Cawley up there. He's one of the deacons."

"Yes'm."

"He hasn't had time to get any kind of commitment papers yet. Still, we don't want any trouble with him. Just stay close to me—both of you—and don't pay him any mind, no matter what he says. Understand?"

I looked at Jeddah. "We understand."

We got out of the car and crossed the driveway. "Take my arm, Jeddah," Eula said, "like you're helping me along. Cam, you get on my other side."

We walked up the gravel path toward the chapel. Ahead, people were gathering around the door. The ladies were talking in soft voices. The men, looking uncomfortable in their Sunday shoes, were hardly talking at all.

We came to the head of the path. "Why, there's Jeddah Whitmire!" one man said. Jeddah beamed and nodded. One lady, tiny and skinny and old, started toward us. "Miss Cornelia," called the girl with her, "you come back here!" The old lady didn't pay her any mind. In quick little steps she came right up to Jeddah, stretched as tall as she could, and kissed him on the cheek.

Jeddah pulled in his chin like an old rooster and stared at her. He must've known her well once—when she was young maybe; maybe even kissed her then—because his face lit up like she'd touched a switch in his mind. He opened his mouth. He seemed ready to say all kinds of things.

Henry Cawley looked up from the ladies he was

welcoming at the door. He dropped their hands and came striding down the walk. "Don't try to talk to him, Miss Cornelia!" he whispered. "He don't have no brain left. It'll only be embarrassing for all concerned." He took her by the shoulders and moved her to the side. "Just pretend he's always been here," he said to everybody.

I wanted to holler that Jeddah was as smart as anybody else, but Eula squeezed my shoulder. Her elbows stiff, she moved us up the walk. Standing aside, Cawley raised his hands like he was the preacher himself. "Come ye in," he said. "Welcome, one and all, to the Church of the Wilderness!"

Once inside the vestibule, we only had a few more steps to reach our pew. Some Bethune in the old days liked to sleep through the services undisturbed, so our family has always sat on the very last row. Eula slipped onto the bench and Jeddah followed her. Just as I was getting ready to sit down by the aisle, Jakie McPhee came up to me. I was glad to see that he had a Band-Aid on his forehead. "This is from Tal," he said, shoving a hymnbook in my hand. Quickly, he went back outside.

A slip of paper was jutting from the gold-edged pages. I pulled it out and read it: *Runt, I ain't finished with you.* I balled it up and jammed it into my pocket.

The chapel was nearly full now. It could hold two hundred and fifty people, and only a few seats were left in the side pews. The Spindales came in and found someone else sitting in their usual places down front. In a huff they sat down across the aisle from us.

The organist began the opening prelude. The choir filed in wearing their wine-colored robes. They sat down together in a raised section behind the pulpit. Above them was the main stained glass window, in the shape of a pointed arch. There were twenty in the choir, and Mama was in the center of the front row. Usually she smiles and nods to people in the congregation. Today she looked pale. She kept her eyes straight ahead.

Henry Cawley and the other deacons marched in. Reverend Healey followed them. He has white hair and a nose that hooks like a beak. His shoulders are wide, his arms long, and his hands are white and huge. He always wears a black suit with wide lapels and two rows of buttons. He keeps a pointed white handkerchief in his breast pocket.

He stepped up to the pulpit and looked out sharply at the congregation. The big wooden arches of the church came to a point high above him. "Let us *pray*."

I bowed my head. I asked God to keep my father safe over in France. I prayed that he'd take care of our other soldiers. I was getting ready to ask him to ease up a little on me, too, when I felt something nudge my leg. I opened my eyes and saw Louise panting up at me.

Jed saw her and held out both hands. Eula laid

her arm across him. "Make her lie down, Cam," she whispered. "Keep her quiet!"

I hunched down in the pew and tried to hold in all her panting and waggling. I made long calm strokes down her back until she finally lay down under the bench. When the prayer ended, I raised my head as if nothing had happened, but I kept my legs tight along her fat sides.

The members of the congregation cleared their throats and settled into their pews as Reverend Healey got ready to read the scripture lesson. He picked 1 Peter 2:11. He read it to us with care, as if he wanted every word to sink in: " 'Dearly beloved, I beseech you as strangers and pilgrims, abstain from fleshly lusts, which war against the soul.' " His voice was calm, but I knew by the end of the service he'd be shouting. His sermons were so full of fire and damnation that each Sunday I expected the sinners in the audience to throw themselves on the altar and beg forgiveness. I'd seen it happen—he'd be shouting and pointing and the choir'd be singing behind him and you'd have to hang on to your pew to keep from running up the aisle toward salvation. The Church of the Wilderness was Episcopal when it first began, and people didn't do that sort of thing. Now it was pure Brimstone. Anything could happen.

Reverend Healey began the sermon by asking the congregation if it knew what fleshly lust was. *"God* knows what it is," he said, "and in the Bible—Galatians, chapter five—he tells us: the curse of man- and

116

womankind is *fornication* and *lasciviousness.*" Those were two new words to me, but by the way he pronounced them I knew they must be pretty bad. His voice went up at the end and his eyes narrowed like he was looking straight into the secret middle of every one of us. Fornica-*shun,* lascivious-*ness.* For all I knew I was wallowing in both of them. Just in case, I stared at a spot on the roof beams so he couldn't read through my eyes and into my heart.

Still keeping his voice low, the reverend began to tell us about couples in the Bible who'd let their fleshly lust get the best of them—Adam and Eve first and foremost. The congregation nodded in agreement and then nodded again for David and Bathsheba and for Samson and Delilah. When he got up to modern times, though, to a woman who'd been a member of his church out in St. Louis, we didn't budge. We knew he was getting to the core of it now, and hellfire was coming.

"She was a beautiful young woman from a fine local family," he said, his voice beginning to rise, "but like Delilah in the Old Testament she was caught up in fleshly lust. She had given herself over to it time and time again. And now, as Peter warns in our scripture lesson, it was torturing her soul. She drank her days away to forget the evil of her nights." His eyes flashed. "In a drunken stupor she even stumbled into my office and put her hands on *me*— God's servant! Like I was her *lover.*"

I felt Jeddah's elbow in my ribs. He opened his

mouth and winked at me, then turned back to the sermon like he didn't want to miss a thing.

"Now," said the reverend, "you might think this woman to be beyond help, so sunken was she. But *no:* Jesus once took pity on a sinner like herself, the cursed *Mary Magdalene,* the Whore of Judea. In search of God's love, I led that woman into a chapel where there was a stained glass window of the Magdalene. She gazed up into that face so much like her own—and lo! At that moment a saintly flash of light, a brilliant sun, shown through that window! *Yes,* my friends, the love of Jesus radiated through the Magdalene's face and onto the very visage of that lost woman! She fell down right there and wept. *Wept!* And from that miraculous moment she was a new and God-fearing soul!" He paused and pointed straight out at us. "And *you,* my flock!" he cried. "What about *you?* Can you be washed in that same light? You *can*—if you let Jesus into your soul!"

He gave a signal to the choir. They began to sing softly in the background. " 'Have thine *own* way, Lord,' " he repeated after them, " 'have thine *own* way.' Are you saying that in your hearts, my people?"

The choir sang, " 'Hold o'er my be-ing ab-so-lute sway . . .' "

"Absolute sway!" he called out. "Like that lost woman, are you ready to let Jesus into every part of you? Are you ready to lie down at his feet?"

I looked over at Jeddah. I thought he'd said something. It didn't sound like "Bet your boots."

"Are you ready," called out the reverend, "to give up your lustful ways—your fornica-*shun,* your lascivious-*ness!*"

" 'While I am wait-ing,' " sang the choir, " 'yield-ed and still-l.' "

"Are you willing? Will you open up yourself to his love?"

"Lies down . . ." mumbled Jeddah.

"Like the bride to the bridegroom!" shouted Reverend Healey. "So the sinner comes to Jesus!"

"Lies down . . ." Jed was actually *talking.* "Puts her legs . . ."

"Jeddah, be quiet!" hissed Eula. He was getting to his feet. I grabbed his arm, but it was too late. "Cam!" he cried. "I know what it is!" The people on the row in front of us twisted around to stare at him. The reverend stopped short; the choir trailed off.

"She lies down," Jeddah said, loud now, all excited, "and opens up her legs. She spreads them legs, Cam, and you pump it to 'er!" He bumped his hips forward. "Hell no, you don't start babies with no *shot.* You do it with your own good ole *weenie!*"

The whole congregation gasped at once. "You hear me, Cam?" Jed cried. "It ain't no doctor that does it! It's *you.* Her hole and your weenie!"

All at once, people were jumping up around us. The ladies covered their ears; their husbands' faces blazed red and angry. Eula pushed me toward the aisle. "Come on, Son," she said. "We gotta get him out of here!"

"You stop *right there!*" It was Henry Cawley, marching up the aisle toward us. "Surely it is clear, my friends," he was saying to the congregation, "that this poor man needs the care and seclusion of an *institution.*"

Louise had waked up in all the commotion. Nervous, twitching around, she saw Cawley coming at us. She gave a shriek and leaped out at him. I threw myself after her and brought her down just short of his feet. Across the aisle Mrs. Spindale screamed. People shouted and grabbed up hymnbooks to protect themselves.

Cawley swayed back against a pew. "Did you *see* that?" he said. "Did you see that bitch *attack* me?"

Quickly, Eula bent down to help me. "Get her out," she whispered. "I'll come after you fast as I can!"

I dragged Louise through the door. Eula pushed Jed after me. Out in the churchyard, running between the tombstones, I heard Cawley shouting behind us: "You're coming home, Jeddah Whitmire! Hear me? You're coming *home!*"

OUT ON THE ROAD Louise stopped to lap from a puddle. She was shivering, looking wild. I was pretty wild myself. "We're in *real* trouble now," I said to Jeddah.

"How come?"

"How come! Cawley just proved you're crazy is how come."

"Shoot," he said, "I ain't crazy."

"I know you ain't crazy, and you know it, but

two hundred and fifty people up that hill think you are!"

"What make 'em to think that?"

"Shouting about weenies and holes is what! In *church.*" I looked at him real close. "You sure it happens that way, Jed? You sure it ain't shots?"

"What ain't shots?"

I waved my arms in the air. *"It!"* I shouted.

The gray coupe roared out of the gate and pulled up beside us. Mama, still in her choir robe, sat beside Eula. "Y'all get in quick," said Eula. "And bring that dog. She looks terrible."

Jed got in next to Mama, and I helped Louise up into his lap. I squeezed in behind them. "Reach out, Jed, and shut the door."

"I'd be most happy to," he said.

"Did you hear how good he can talk?" I said.

"The whole *church* did!" said Eula. She gave him one of her looks and let out the clutch.

As we sped off, Mama put a handkerchief to her eyes. "This has been the most awful Sunday of my life," she said.

"Now, Bess," said Eula, "nobody actually got hurt, and they haven't got Jeddah yet. We can be thankful for that."

"I don't mean that." She looked around at me. Her eyes were quivering. "I mean the preacher talking about me in his sermon."

"What . . . ?" I said.

"Why, honey," said Eula, "he wasn't talking about you."

"Ohhh, yes, he was! He didn't say right out, 'Bess Reed is a *sinner*,' but he might as well have. Making all those references to me and Henry. 'Lasciviousness' and all. He practically wrote 'Magdalene' on my forehead!"

"If that ain't true about you and Henry," said Eula, "then you got nothing to be ashamed of."

"*Course* it ain't true!" I shouted.

"Course it ain't!" said Mama. "I mean 'isn't.' " She burst out crying. She pushed Louise toward Jeddah so she'd have more room. "*Ohh!*" she cried, jerking her hand back. "She's having contractions. She's gonna have her puppies right in this car!"

"Is that right, Jed?" I said.

"Reckon it is."

Eula told everybody to hang on to their hats. She jammed her foot on the gas. In minutes we were swerving into the driveway back home. We rolled up to the front porch, and I jumped out to help Louise down. "Let me out of here too," said Mama. "I can't stand one more thing this morning." Jeddah didn't move from the seat. "You help," he said to her.

"With the puppies? Eula knows better than I do."

"I'll help too," said Eula. "But Louise is old. We oughta all be out there."

"But I—"

"Go on with Jeddah. I'll be right out."

Mama put her hand to her temple. "Oh, my Lord," she said.

Louise's box was in the back yard beside the toolshed. Panting nervously, she waddled around the side of the house toward it. I stayed beside her. Jed took Mama's elbow and followed us. When Lyda saw us coming, she leaned out the kitchen door and said, "Look like everything happen at once 'round here. I'm gon' fix everybody some ice tea!" Mama called to her that she'd fix the tea, but Jed kept hold of her arm.

Sighing, Mama slumped down on the toolhouse steps. She unsnapped the collar of her robe. "This is the worst headache in human memory."

Louise was panting crazily now. Rolling her eyes, she shivered, drank from her bowl. She paced around and around the box. Desperately, she hobbled into it and lay down. Her sides started to heave. A wet sack began slowly squeezing out of her body. You could actually see the shape of the little puppy inside. I held Jeddah's hand. "Ain't she something, Jed!"

When the sack was all the way out, she turned around and opened it with her teeth. She seemed a little surprised to find a pup inside. Still, she knew what to do. She licked it clean, carefully bit off the cord to its belly, and nudged it with her nose.

"Why doesn't it move?" I said.

"What's the matter?" said Mama from the steps.

I put my hands over my ears. "Is something the matter?"

Jeddah knelt down and picked up the pup. It was so tiny he could hold it in the palm of one hand. He lifted it to his ear. He mashed its sides, listened to it, mashed it again and then again. Slowly, he stood up. He took off his coat and spread it on a grassy bank beside the shed. He lay the puppy on it and folded the coat across it.

"Cam, come here, honey," said Mama.

I went to the coat instead, thinking they must be wrong. I unfolded the blue cloth, but the little dog was dead.

"Jeddah, she's having another one," said Mama.

The second sack came out quickly. It held a second pup with no heartbeat. Jeddah pressed its sides, but nothing helped. He put it under his coat with the other one. "You didn't tell me they'd be dead," I said, stepping back. "You didn't tell me that."

"Cam, he didn't know," said Mama.

"I don't care!" I walked down the hill toward the house so they wouldn't see me cry.

I felt like I was choking. I'd never really known that something you loved could die. If that was true, then Daddy could get killed; Hitler could win. Henry Cawley could take Jed away. He could take Mama.

I looked back at them. Jed had sat down beside the shed. He was staring at the ground. He seemed exhausted. Mama told him another puppy was coming, but he didn't look up.

"I think it's the last one," she said. She knelt beside the box. "Jeddah, this one's not breathing either." She looked up at him. "Won't you try to save it?" He didn't seem to hear her. "Eula!" she called. "Where *is* everybody?"

She picked up the new pup and cradled it in her hands. She stared at it for a moment, then put it quickly to her ear. Scrambling up, she held it out to Jeddah. "The heart's beating. Maybe just the windpipe is blocked." She pushed the puppy into his hands. "Listen!" she cried. She hit the side of his neck. *"Listen* to me! We can't let all Cam's puppies die!"

Jeddah gazed up at her uncertainly. "Please try," she said. She pulled him to his feet. She held him steady till he got his balance. He swallowed hard and looked down the hill at me. He seemed so old. Slowly, he held the little dog out in front of him. Like some ancient Indian, he raised it above his head. For what seemed like forever he stood there, trembling, frail against the sky. Suddenly, in a sure curve he swung it down, stopping sharply at his knees. Startled, the pup gasped for air.

"Oh, *yes!"* cried Mama. Bending down, she took it from him and held it up for me to see. It wiggled sleepily. Shouting, I ran back. "You did it, Jed!"

He stepped back against the toolhouse. He was pulling air into his lungs just like the puppy. "I did," he said.

THE PUPPY WAS A BOY. He was mostly brown, like Louise, but he had a black stripe down his back and one beautiful white ear. His eyes were still closed tight, as if he didn't want to see what a strange place he had ended up in.

Jed and I hung around him all Sunday afternoon, telling each other how grand he was. The only one who wasn't really thrilled was Louise. Every time the pup started nosing around the nipples on her stomach, she got this long-suffering look on her face, like she'd rather be anywhere in the world than in that box. Jeddah laughed at her and said she was normal.

Mama stayed in her room. Only once, when Jed and I left the puppy for a while, did she come down. She went out back and sat alone beside the box. I could see her from the kitchen window. She was stroking Louise very gently. When she came in, she went back upstairs without speaking to anybody. I heard Eula go to her door and ask her if she could help, but Mama said no. I wanted to help her, too, but something stubborn kept us apart.

Jed talked the whole afternoon. He seemed to be making up for all the time he hadn't said anything. One of the things he came up with was a name for the puppy—Jefferson after Jefferson Davis, the President of the Confederacy. I had a better one. "I want to call him J.W.," I said, "for Jeddah Whitmire."

He looked pleased. "Okay."

"J.W.," I repeated. "Sounds nice and military. Were you ever in the army, Jed?"

He shook his head. "Always too old."

"Too old . . . ? When were you born?"

Jeddah's mind still skipped a beat now and then, and it took him a while to come up with the date: 1862. "Good gravy," I said, "you mean you were alive during the War Between the States?"

"I'm pretty sure. I know my papa fought at the First Battle of . . . lemme see . . ."

"Manassas?"

"That's the one. I remember the day he came home after the war. First time I'd ever seen him. Thought he looked like a scarecrow."

"Was he wounded?"

"Seems like he was . . . bullet in his leg, right about here. Made him walk funny."

"What else?" I said.

"What else, what?"

"What else about your *daddy*, Jed."

"Well . . ." He scratched his head. "I remember Mama grabbed me up and ran out to meet him. He hugged us, said we were the best thing he'd seen in four years." He chuckled. "I was scared of him. Socked him on the jaw. He laughed till he cried. Cried all the way into the house and then laughed and then cried all over again. Mama too."

"You remember that after all these years?"

"If I jog my head enough. You'll remember it, too, when it's your papa coming home."

Daddy coming home. . . . I'd always thought I couldn't wait for that moment, but now things had changed. I could see him walking up, hearing about Mama, glancing around at me, fierce: *Why didn't you do something, Cam?*

"Jed," I said, "you know Cawley's gonna be coming for you soon."

He looked at me blankly. "What for?"

"Don't you remember? To take you back to the Home."

"Oh."

"He's coming and I—" I peered at Jed, wishing he'd tell me what to do, but he was waiting for me to say. "Well, I—I'll just hide you, that's all."

The only place I could think of that Cawley couldn't find was the old cabin where I'd first seen Jed. He could duck into the orchard when we heard Cawley drive up, and I could smuggle him out to the cabin at night. If Adolf Hitler was planning to hide out in these mountains, then they ought to be secret enough for me and Jed.

I told him about it, but all he said was, "That old brokedown place?" He seemed insulted.

"Well, you went there after you left Cawley's, didn't you? You must've wanted to then."

"Never had laid eyes on that dump in my life." He hooked his thumb over at the box. "It was her idea."

Louise looked back at us dumbly, surprised that we were talking about her. "You mean she led you there?" I said.

"If it wasn't her, I don't know who it was. All I remember is just ..." He hesitated. He raised his chin. Obstinately, he stuck out his lower lip.

"What, Jed?"

His jaw quavered. "All I remember," he said, "is

one day finding out my daughter was dead. She'd been gone a month . . . and they hadn't told me. My sweet daughter."

"Jed, I'm awful sorry."

"Well . . . it broke my heart, is all. Felt like I didn't have nothing left. Nothing left to feel . . . nothing left to say. Just sat outside the Home and stared at the woods. Day in and day out."

He rubbed his hand across the wrinkles in his forehead. "I musta been near 'bout crazy. Started seeing some kind of face staring back at me from the trees. Some kind of wolf-ghost." He reached over to the box and touched Louise. "Kept coming back, like she was waiting to lead me off to Darkness." He sniffed hard, then spit out into the yard. "I didn't care anymore. Stepped through a broke place in the fence, followed her into the forest. Thought I was already a dead man. On my way to Darkness."

I said, "I'm glad you didn't die, Jed."

"Well . . . there wasn't much reason not to. Till you came rolling up to my feet. White as another ghost."

"I was pretty scared."

"The scaredest boy I'd ever seen."

I picked up J.W. from the box. I stood up and held him high above my head, like Jeddah had done when he was born. His little face looked grumpy against the clouds. I laughed. "He's no ghost, Jed."

"Me neither," he said. "Not yet anyhow."

131

I put the puppy back beside Louise. He snuggled against her stomach and began to nurse again. I squatted to watch. "How long does it take for a dog to have puppies?" I said.

"Ain't right sure. Takes folks nine months."

"Nine months from the time they do it till the time the baby comes out?"

"Yep." He started chuckling, and I said, "What're you laughing at?"

"Oh, just thinking 'bout doing it. Trying to remember when the last time was."

"But you just had one daughter, didn't you?" I said. "So you only did it one time, right?"

Jed slapped his leg. "What you talking 'bout, boy? One time!"

I felt myself get red in the face. "Well, but . . . you only do it to have a baby, don't you?"

"Wha-at! Son, you do it every chance you get! You think your mama and papa only did it one time? Course when you're planning on it you can have a baby—like they had you—but most times you just do it for good ole bare-ass *fun.*"

I turned my head away and thought about what he'd said. "Jeddah," I said, not looking at him, "you think Mama would ever do it with anybody besides Daddy?"

"Huh . . . ?"

"You know. You think she'd do it with somebody else—maybe just for fun?"

Jeddah sat back, astounded. "Where'd you think *that* up?"

"Well, what the preacher said. . . ."

"Nawww. Forget what the preacher said."

"You sure?"

"Course I'm sure. I been seeing your mama and papa most of their lives. 'Fore they met each other they had lots of sweethearts. But after that they never *thought* about anybody else."

"I'm talking about now."

"Then *and* now." He touched my shoulder to make sure I was paying attention. "I remember one night I saw 'em walking down the street over in Hendersonville after a movie. They'd been married quite a while, but they were strolling along holding hands like they were sixteen years old. He'd lean down and whisper something, and she'd laugh and bounce her hip over against his."

"Maybe she was just flirting."

"Sure she was flirting. But the important thing is they *loved* each other. And when you love somebody like that, you don't wanta do it with anybody else. I don't care how much fun it'd be."

"But I've seen her flirt with Cawley too."

"Shoot. Everybody flirts."

"Yeah, but—"

"Listen, when you see your papa and mama together again, you study 'em like I did. You gonna see nothing but love."

"Are you *sure*, Jed?"

He grinned. "Bet your boots."

☆   ☆

Sunday was almost over when it happened.

We'd eaten supper early and put the dishes away. Eula and Mama had gone to their bedrooms. Jed had walked out back to check one last time on Louise. I was waiting for him in front of the big floor-model radio in the living room.

I listened as war news came on: our men in the Pacific were struggling to take Saipan Island; in France they were fighting to capture Cherbourg. A late bulletin said that winged one-ton bombs were flying into England. Terrible, they made a buzzing sound as they passed. The buzz went silent just before they crashed and exploded. "There is little doubt," said the commentator, "that this is Hitler's dreaded secret weapon."

I clicked off the radio and walked out to the front hall. The door to the porch was open, and I could see a red sky outside. It had rained earlier. Now the last of the sun glinted through the fan window above the door.

I started up the stairs. I hesitated: a smell, a feeling, something. . . . I whirled around. Henry Cawley stood in the doorway. I couldn't move. In that second the Packard pulled up to the porch. A Negro man in an orderly's coat was driving. Tal was beside him.

I vaulted down the stairs and ran for the back yard. "Jeddah!" I shouted, bursting from the house. "Hide!" He was standing beside Louise's box. A sad, puzzled look spread over his face. Louise leaped up. Her hackles high, she planted herself in front of him.

"He ain't gonna hide nowhere!" yelled Tal. He and the orderly were right behind me. Tal dived for my legs and threw me down. Damp grass stuck to our arms. We rolled over, but he seemed even bigger than the last time. He got his legs around my back and pinned me against the ground.

Cawley strode out of the house stuffing official-looking papers into his vest pocket. Eula, wearing her housecoat, was right with him. "Henry Cawley," she said, "I don't care *what* those papers say! You get off my property this minute, and take these henchmen of yours with you!"

"In good time, Mrs. Bethune." He headed straight for Jeddah. Louise growled threateningly. She moved toward him. "Look out, Daddy!" shouted Tal.

"Hush up, Son." He made a sign to the orderly. The man came up beside him with a heavy net in his hands.

Louise flicked her eyes from one to the other. Cawley dodged to the left. She went for him, and the orderly flung the net across her. Howling, she tried to leap out of it, but her paws caught in the mesh. She fell helplessly onto her back. Keeping out of range of her teeth, the man pulled it around her and tied the ends together. She howled crazily inside. "That takes care of her," said Tal. He dug his heels into my sides.

Jeddah hadn't moved since they came into the yard. All at once, he raised his arms and rushed at Cawley. He grabbed him by the neck. "Get back here!" Cawley yelled to the orderly. The man ran to Jeddah, swung him around, pinned his arms behind him. "Don't you hurt him!" I cried.

Cawley stepped back, breathing hard. "He's just overwrought," he said. "Comes from living in the wrong conditions!" He stepped up to Jeddah. "Relax . . . relax now. Everything's all right." Jeddah worked his throat furiously. He opened his mouth to speak, but all the fight had drained from him. He panted, trying to catch his breath. "There, there," said Cawley. He told the orderly to let him go. He patted Jeddah's shoulder and began to steer him toward the front yard. "Let this be a lesson to you, Mrs. Bethune!"

"Henry, you're *always* a lesson to me," said Eula. She reached down to Tal and yanked him off me. "And so is this hooligan." She sent him spinning toward his father.

I scrambled to my feet and grabbed her arm. "Can't you stop 'em, Eula?"

"They got the papers, son. All signed by the county magistrate."

"Mr. Spindale . . . !"

"It's the law," called out Cawley. "And we're

obliged to obey it." He ushered Jed around the corner of the house.

"Eula, Eula!" I cried.

She put both her hands over mine. "Son . . . ! I'm sorry!"

I broke away and ran through the house to the front porch. They were just coming around to the car. In the fading light I saw someone else standing beside it. It was Mama.

"Evening, Bess," Cawley said. "I know this is an unpleasantness, but—"

She interrupted him. "Henry, I have something for you." She held out a slim package wrapped in cellophane. It was the pair of stockings he had given her. She slapped it down on the fender of the car. In the still evening it sounded like the crack of a rifle. "You'll find they've been opened, but that was purely by accident. They have never touched my skin."

"Bess, you don't have—"

"Not *once,*" she said. She turned her back and stepped up onto the porch beside me. She put her arm on my shoulder and pulled me close against her side. She was trembling. I braced her with my arm. It seemed a long time since we'd held each other. "Henry," she said, "you are no longer welcome in this house."

"But, Bess . . . !"

"I mean it," she said.

He gave her a long look. Finally, dropping his

shoulders in disgust, he told the orderly to put Jeddah in the car. As they held the door for him, Jed glanced at us. The blankness was back in his eyes. I wasn't sure he even understood what was happening. His shoulders looked so thin.

Cawley waited till they were all inside, then took his place at the wheel. He started the engine and put the car in gear. After making a circle around the pool, he set out down the driveway.

Eula came to the screen door behind us. Louise, free from the net, was whining beside her. Eula opened the door and Louise skittered across the porch and down the steps. She raced after the car. Catching up with it, she ran barking beside Jeddah's window. There were shallow puddles in the clay of the drive. She charged through them, splashing muddy water behind her.

Cawley swung out onto the paved highway. Louise tried to keep up, but the Packard was soon beyond her. She glanced back at the Arbor in confusion. Slowly she came to a halt. Ears low, she watched the car disappear down the road.

AR ISN'T MEDALS AND victories," Daddy wrote me. "It's a terrible thing, Cam, full of dying and suffering. And there's no such thing as a hero. I know you and Charlie think I'm a hero, but the truth is I'm scared most of the time. All of us are. And sick to death of what we have to do. The really brave ones in this world are people like Jeddah Whitmire—living his own life, right to the end. I'm glad you're helping him. Tell him I'm on his side too."

I read the letter to Mama. She cried and said, "They're both heroes. Pat and Jeddah both."

But Jed was gone.

I tried everything I could think of to take my mind off his leaving—I built a doghouse, I helped Lyda with the dishes, I tagged after Eula everywhere she went. I must've driven her to distraction, but she always had time to tell me not to worry. Jeddah was stronger than he looked, she said, and it would take more than Henry Cawley to get him down.

Mama went each day to Hendersonville to take a first-aid course at the Red Cross. An instruction manual came with the course, and she read a part of it to me every night. She put together an emergency kit of cotton swabs, mercurochrome, tape, gauze, and enough ammonia to revive a battalion. "We are in a war, son," she said, as if she'd just discovered it, "and we all have to do our part." She also had two private talks with Reverend Healey. I heard Eula grumble that there was nothing worse than a reformed sinner, but I liked this new Mama.

I got Eula to telephone the Cawley Home each morning and ask if Jeddah could have visitors. They always told her no. He was getting readjusted, they said, and they didn't want outsiders to spoil it. Eula told me to be patient, but I couldn't. After a week I made up my mind to go whether they allowed it or not.

I waited till midafternoon, when I knew the orderlies let the old folks walk around the grounds. If I was careful, I could slip through the fence and see Jed without being discovered. Not telling anyone where I was going, I put J.W. inside my shirt and walked along the highway toward Cawley's. Louise trotted beside me, ears up, knowing something important was happening.

When we got near Cogswell's Grocery, Charlie saw me from the porch and waved me up. "Cam Reed," he said, putting down his broom. "I haven't seen you in a long time. What's kept you away?"

"Oh, just things. . . ."

"Well, I been missing you. Are you doing all right?"

"I guess so."

"What's that in your shirt?"

I lifted out J.W. "This is Louise's puppy," I said, putting him on the floor. "Named J.W. after Jeddah Whitmire, who saved his life."

Charlie squatted down beside him and stroked his head with the back of his finger. J.W. gnawed on him sleepily. "I heard about that," he said. "Your mama told me old Jed was just about the best doctor she'd ever seen. 'Inspiring' is what she called him."

I heard a giggle inside the store. Looking up, I saw Tal behind the screen door. Rob and Jakie were standing beside him. "Hey, Cam," Tal said, not at all unfriendly. "That your new puppy?"

I just nodded and began to gather up J.W.

"Hold on, Cam," said Charlie. "You boys oughta be friends again. Come on, let 'em pet this cute thing. Cutest thing I ever seen. Got one white ear."

The three of them stepped out onto the porch and squatted beside us. They stroked J.W. and said I sure was lucky to have such a nice pet. It made me nervous to see them so friendly. Louise didn't like it either. I said I had to go. "Where to?" said Tal.

"Oh . . . just around. You know, to show J.W. around." I picked him up and tucked him in next to my stomach. As I walked off, Charlie called after me to come again soon. I looked back and said I would. Charlie was still on the porch, but the boys were gone.

I shrugged. I wouldn't figure Tal out if I lived to be as old as Jeddah. I turned onto the road that led to the Cawley Home. A white wooden sign with black iron curlicues around it said "Rest for the Aged—One Mile Ahead." It looked like directions to Heaven, but I knew better.

The road wound slowly up a hill. As we turned a bend, the Cawley tower came into view above the treetops. Its sides were covered with gray and black shingles that made a diamond pattern around it. The shingles on the roof were solid black. A lightning rod pointed sharply out of the peak.

I got a sinking feeling in my stomach. I remembered all the terrible things I'd heard—the poisoned millionaire, the skulls, Charlie's white-haired cousin. I began to wish I'd waited till Eula and Mama could come with me. Louise walked stiffly beside my legs, as if she were uneasy too.

A gateway blocked the road ahead. It was connected to a high metal fence that disappeared into the forest on both sides. Before the guard could see me, I stepped off the road into the trees. I circled the property beside the fence. Through it I could see the Home. It sat in the middle of a flat grassy yard. It was big and sprawling and covered with gray wooden shingles. There were gables all around the third story, some with arched windows and balconies. All the trim was painted dark maroon. Along the front porch were heavy maroon posts and railings with dark wire screening stretched between them. It looked like the setting for one of Eulalee's mystery novels.

I could see old folks behind the screen. I counted fifteen, almost the entire population of the Home, but none of them was Jeddah. I followed the fence to the back of the building. This was the part that Cawley had closed off when he bought the mansion. Here, the windows were shuttered, and weeds sprouted against the brick foundation. In the middle of the rear wing a low ramp led up to a door that looked like it hadn't been opened in years. A gabled roof was above it. Beyond that rose the tower.

Jed was sitting on a bench at the far end of the back yard, looking out at the forest. An orderly was sitting nearby in a folding chair. Louise saw Jed and began to quiver.

While we watched, the orderly got up and

stretched. He looked around with a bored expression. Checking his watch, he sighed and walked around the house to the front yard.

Quickly, I found the break in the fence that Jeddah had told me about and slipped through it with Louise. We were only a few yards from him, but we were still hidden by bushes and trees. I hissed out, "Jed!" The sound triggered Louise. She shot forward, circled Jeddah, her paws sending the grass flying, and dashed back in under the bushes. Jeddah looked around, amazed.

"Jed!" I whispered again. "It's me!" He stared at us. Slowly, he smiled and raised his hand. I pointed at a stump beside our bush. He came over and sat down on it. "Look," I said, "I brought J.W." Jed picked him up and petted him, but his eyes didn't light up like I hoped they would. After a minute he handed him back to me.

"Jed, you doing okay?"

He nodded. "I . . . am okay." His voice was rusty, like it had been at the cabin, and I knew he hadn't been talking at all. I told him about the doghouse I'd built and about Mama's first-aid course, but nothing seemed to interest him. He nodded and said a few things, but most of the time he just sat there. He seemed years older and a hundred miles away from the Arbor.

It made me so sad to see him like that. I got up and told him I was going to take a walk. It was just an excuse to be alone for a few minutes, to think what I ought to do. Louise stayed with him. I wandered between the trees, still inside the fence, yet hidden from both Jed and the orderlies around front. I'd only been gone a few minutes when a voice behind me said, "Cam."

I pivoted around and saw Rob Aiken smirking at me. "Scared you, huh?"

"N-naw," I said. "Something musta bit me." I scratched my neck to show what I meant.

He snickered and said, "Is that J.W. in your shirt?"

"Yeah, that's him."

"Can I hold him?"

"I don't know . . ." I started edging back in the direction of Jeddah.

"Oh, come on," he said. "I won't hurt him."

"Well, just for a minute. Then I gotta go. We're not supposed to be here."

He took J.W. and held him up to his cheek. "He sure is soft."

"Yeah, he is. Well . . ."

"Tal was telling me one of the old ladies here at the Home really wants to see your puppy." He backed away. "Come on, let's go show him to her."

He began to trot off with J.W. tucked under his arm. "Naw, Rob!" I ran after him, but he speeded up. He stayed just inside the trees. Suddenly he veered across the grass to the ramp that led to the old back door. He ran up it, jerked open the door, and disappeared inside.

Dumbfounded, I stopped at the edge of the trees. Didn't he know about the tower? I looked around for help, but Jeddah was way at the end of the yard. He was staring off into nothing again. I didn't see Louise. And I knew I couldn't call the orderlies.

Taking a deep breath, I ran across the grass and up the ramp. I stepped through the door. An empty hallway stretched in front of me. The only light struggled in through breaks in the shutters along the left wall. On the right, doors opened into rooms that looked like black caves. At the far end was the bottom of a staircase.

I heard footsteps climbing the stairs. They were already high along it. "Rob Aiken!" I shouted. "Come back here!" My voice bounced off the bare walls. "Don't you know where this is?"

I ran to the stairs. I clutched the huge, dusty newel post and peered above me. Rob had disappeared, leaving the stair deserted. It spiraled silently into the darkness. I knew the tower room was at the top—where wars and terrors had been plotted, where skeletons still hung. And J.W. was up there! I yelled, "Rob, come back down quick!" but my chest tightened and my voice came out pale and weak. I could hardly breathe.

I backed away from the post. My legs bumped something that moved and screeched, and I fell back against the steps. An old wheelchair rolled across the floor in front of me. Embarrassed, I kicked out at it.

Holding on to the newel post, I pulled myself up. This time I didn't look above me. I put my foot on the first step, then stepped up again. The stair creaked under my shoes. The treads were crusty with droppings. I slid my palm along the wide wooden bannister. Layers of dust, older than I was, piled up in front of my hand.

I wondered if Charlie's cousin Wilson had been this frightened when he climbed the tower. He'd ended up with white hair and no feeling in his fingers. I heard a rush of wings. Black shapes flicked past me. I began to think Wilson had gotten off easy. . . .

There were no landings on the stairs. I could only edge higher and higher along the curving rail. The air grew dense and musty as I climbed. It had a heavy, choking smell. Somehow I knew it was the smell of war—of the dying and suffering that Daddy had written me about. *It's a terrible thing, Cam. . . . We're scared most of the time. And sick to death of what we have to do. . . .*

I felt the stairs end. A heavy paneled door appeared in the shadows before me. As I stood in front of it, the brass handle began to turn. Inch by inch, the door moved back on its hinges. I could see the outline of a small round room beyond it. It was almost completely dark. Its one window was shrouded in heavy black cloth.

147

Suddenly a match flared in the middle of the room. The wick of a candle caught fire. It spread flickering light across the top of a wooden table. J.W. lay on the table, whimpering and afraid.

Behind the flame stood a huge man dressed in black. A red swastika glowed on his arm. Deliberately, he picked up the candle and raised it to his chin: a square mustache, maddened eyes, a slash of black hair. . . .

"Oh, Lord," I whispered, "Adolf Hitler!"

BLACK FIGURES PULLED
me into the room and held me out toward Hitler.
Eyes burning, I looked up into his face.

Incredibly, his mustache began to wiggle. A giggle slipped from his lips. It grew to a belly laugh. He
whipped a black cloth from his body. Only Tal was
left, teetering on an apple basket.

Rob and Jakie pulled off their hoods. Bent over
laughing, they fell on a row of big pillows against the

wall. Tal squalled, "Oh, Lord—Adolf Hitler!" and the laughter started all over again.

I was shaking and confused, but more than anything I was mad: you don't pretend to be Hitler! I dived for Tal. I got a good punch in his stomach before Rob and Jakie leaped up and pinned me to the wall. "Not so fast!" they said.

Brushing himself off, Tal pretended I hadn't hurt him. He reached into a drawer under the table. "We figured you might get outta hand," he said, "so we brought these along." He held up something long and filmy. "Don't you recognize 'em? They're those nylons your mama likes so much."

"Dammit, Tal . . . !"

"Shut up," growled Jakie. He bent my arms behind me. I twisted and fought, but they tied my wrists together with one of the stockings. "Dammit, Tal," I cried, "lemme loose!"

He poked me in the chest. With my arms behind me, I couldn't keep my balance. I fell into the pillows. Rob jumped on top of me and tied the other stocking around my ankles.

"That oughta take care of you," said Tal. He went back to the table, picked up J.W., and put him in a basket on the floor. From the drawer he took a pack of Lucky Strikes. He slipped one under his mustache and lit it.

"Big deal," I said. "I seen you smoke before."

Tal wagged his head from side to side. "It ain't a

big deal when *I* smoke," he said, "but it is when *you* do." He held it out to me.

Rob took the Lucky and poked it at my lips. He held my nose till I gasped, then forced the tip into my mouth. His fingers went in, too, and I bit down. "Owww!" he hollered. He rolled back against the pillows, the cigarette flying from his hand. "You're gonna pay for that!" He stood up, ready to kick me.

Tal reached out and stopped him. He grinned at me. "Tough little runt, ain'tcha?"

"Tougher'n you, Tal Cawley!"

"And you're real grown up. Know all there is about sex, don't you?"

I hesitated and then said, "Sure."

"Well, tell you what I'm gonna do. When you let us in on all the stuff that old man's been telling you about sex, we'll let you go."

"Uh . . . what stuff about sex?"

They all guffawed. "All that talk about 'pumping it to her.' We heard him in church. He musta told you a lot more since then."

Jakie wrinkled his nose. "Being that old geezer, it musta all been dirty too." He moved in closer on the pillows. "Let's hear it."

"He didn't tell me anything 'cept how babies get started," I said. "And that ain't dirty."

"The hell it ain't!" sneered Jakie.

I kicked out at him. "The hell it is!"

He rolled out of range, then got a surprised look

on his face. He started bouncing across the floor. "Yow!" he shouted. He jumped up, pounding the back of his trousers. I looked where he'd been and saw the cigarette smoldering in one of the pillows. "Stomp it out," said Rob. Jakie kicked at the pillow, but that only mashed it like a bellows, making the embers jump into flame.

"Move," said Tal. "Lemme have it." He took a corner and walked with it to the window. Yanking the black cloth away, he flung the pillow out toward the yard, but one side knocked against the window frame and it spun onto the roof below. "No," said Tal, backing into the middle of the room. "Oh, no!"

Rob grabbed a half-full Nehi from the corner. He poured it from the window. "That don't help!" he cried. "It's catching the shingles."

Smoke was already drifting up past the room. "Come on," said Tal. "We gotta climb out there. We gotta put it out!"

"Hell no," said Rob, starting for the door. "I'm getting outta here. This old place'll go up like a matchbox!"

"He's right," said Jakie.

"*Stop.*" Tal blocked the doorway, his hands on his hips. "You take orders from *me.*"

"But, Tal—"

"I'm the *dictator.*"

They hesitated one more second before shoving him away. Their footsteps clattered on the stairs. Tal tried to yell after them, but no sounds came out. His Hitler mustache trembled against his pale skin. He stretched out his arms and turned in a circle, like he was reaching for help.

"Untie me, Tal!" I cried. "I'll help put it out!" Not seeming to hear me, he picked up another pillow and leaned out the window to batter the flames. Smoke billowed around him and he fell back coughing.

"Tal!" I shouted. "You gotta *untie* me!" He weaved across the room and dropped to his knees beside me. He was coughing hard, blinking his eyes. *"Untie* me!" I said. "Hurry!"

He fumbled with the knot at my ankles. His head began to wobble. "Cam . . . !" His eyes fluttered and he slumped across my legs.

I looked at the window. *"Help!"* I shouted, trying to direct my voice through it. Smoke poured in to block it. Flames skipped up the wooden frame, sending sharp heat across the floor.

I rolled out from under Tal. Bending my legs, I pushed myself toward the wall like a snake. I got my back against it and managed to sit up. I pulled my legs in under me. Little by little, I edged up till I was standing.

It was so smoky I had to bend over again to breathe. I hopped in the direction of the door. If I could get to the stairs . . .

Out of the corner of my eye I saw Tal. He was

lying face down on the floor, helpless. I stared at him. I knew he was mean and awful, but he'd been my friend. I heard a whimpering sound. The basket beside the table began to wobble. I'd forgotten J.W. too!

Heaving myself around, I started back to them. My feet caught in one of the pillows and I lost my balance. I crashed down; my head hit the floor. I struggled to get up again, but the room was spinning around me. . . .

A sudden darkness filled my head. Far within it a soft line began to glimmer. The line widened and stretched into a horizon. It became mountains and soaring clouds. It moved toward me, adding rolling slopes and orchards. On the closest hillside I saw the Arbor—its white arches, the round pool in the drive, the long meadow that leads to the road. And all at once I knew I was looking out from the rock above Pinehill again. All the things I loved were there. I heard Louise barking from the trail below. She was coming up to meet me on the rock . . . sweet Louise . . . I was glad she'd be with me. . . .

I felt a cold nose on my cheek, a rough tongue against my face. As I moved away from them, the view in my head began to evaporate. I saw the tower room again. It was glowing like a smoky furnace. The silhouette of a wolf hovered over me. "Louise . . . ?"

She poked my side with her snout, then bounded across the floor to the basket that held J.W. I heard a noise on the stairs. Horribly drowsy, I rolled my head toward the door. Through the smoke I saw Jeddah lope breathlessly into the room. "Lord, boy," he said, finding me, "you gotta get outta here!"

"Oh, Jed . . ."

"Hurry, boy!"

I was fighting sleep. "I can't," I said. "I'm tied up in ladies' nylons."

"Ladies' *what?*"

"And Tal . . . and J.W. . . ."

"Lord have mercy!" Hands shaking, he found the knots on my wrists. He loosened them enough for me to slip my arms free. As if in a dream, I reached for the band at my ankles. I forced my fingers to work it apart.

Jeddah sat Tal up and tried to lift him, but he was too heavy. "We got to do it together," he said. "Can you stand up, boy?"

"I . . . I think so. . . ." Unsteadily, I got to my feet. I picked up one of Tal's legs. Jed took the other and we struggled with him out to the landing. Louise was already on the stairs, J.W.'s basket between her teeth.

There was less smoke in the stairwell, but the fire had surrounded the tower, and slivers of red were showing through the cracks in the plaster. Coughing, Jeddah sagged against the wall. "Hang him over the rail," he croaked.

Together we saddled Tal across the curving

bannister. His legs were on our side; his upper body hung loosely over into the stairwell. We hooked our hands into his belt to keep him from falling. Slowly we started down, me in front, stumbling backward, Jed behind like an anchor. I felt hot ashes on my arms, and I knew the blaze had eaten through the roof. The whole inside of the stairwell was bright now with fiery light. Over Jed's shoulder I saw the tower room explode in flames. They leaped out into the landing above us.

I heard an awful tearing sound. The stairs began to weave under my feet. They swayed away from the wall. Tal's body shifted on the bannister. "Hold him!" shouted Jeddah. I threw my arms across Tal's back. My feet slipped, and I lurched over the railing. I looked down into the red well of the tower. My head began to swim, and I felt the darkness coming back.

Jeddah grabbed my collar. He pulled me back onto the tottering stairs. "Don't give up, son!"

I looked up into his face. There were ashes on his forehead; his cheeks were streaked with soot and sweat. He was old and he was frightened, but there was a light in his eyes as strong as the fire around us. Jeddah Whitmire was alive!

"I won't, Jed," I said. "I won't!"

With pieces of the burning roof falling around us, we inched Tal down the bannister. I could hear Louise barking below us, but I didn't look down again. I walked backward, keeping my eyes on Jed.

I didn't know I'd reached the bottom until the bannister ended and Tal slid off into my arms. Jeddah ran past me to the wheelchair I'd bumped into earlier. He pushed it up to us. "Sit him down!"

A huge crunch sounded overhead. A beam fell from the ceiling and crashed onto the stairs. Another fell right after it, tumbling toward us. Embers flew like shrapnel. Jed shouted for me to run. Through the smoke I saw Louise barking in the open door at the end of the corridor. I ran toward her. In a moment I was pitching down the ramp onto the cool grass at the bottom.

I looked up to see Jed rolling Tal through the door. He was gasping for breath, but his head was up, his wispy hair was flying. He had saved us!

☆   ☆

Orderlies ran from the front yard and pulled us away from the house. They were all apologizing at once: they had gotten the residents out of the building as soon as they'd smelled smoke, but they'd had no idea anyone was in the tower. "How'd you know, Mr. Whitmire?" they said. Jed pointed at Louise. She was guarding J.W. at the edge of the trees.

"It was her."

In the front yard the old people crowded around us, wiping our faces, brushing ashes from our hair. Henry Cawley rushed up to Tal's wheelchair. "Son!

Son!" he cried, slapping Tal's wrists. Slowly Tal opened his eyes and saw his father. "I'm sorry, Daddy," he whispered.

Cawley put his arms around him and bowed his head. When he looked up, his eyes were moist. "You saved my boy," he said to Jeddah. "I saw you, you saved my boy."

The fire truck from Hendersonville burst into the yard, bells clanging. Cawley hurried to direct it. Right behind it came Eula in her coupe. She jolted to a stop inches short of a fireman. Mama jumped out, her medical kit in her hand. She spotted us across the yard and realized we were the victims. She looked ready to faint. "Get blankets!" she cried, running toward us.

When she reached us, I said, "Tal's worst."

"Oh, my Lord!" she cried, staring at him. "His upper lip is charred!"

Feebly, Tal reached up and peeled off his Hitler disguise. "It's just my mustache," he said.

Mama pulled out a huge bottle of ammonia. She took a quick whiff herself before holding it under Tal's nose. She administered it to Jeddah then, and to me, and on to everybody in sight. She spread blankets and made all three of us lie down. She put pillows under our feet and covered us with more blankets.

When everyone was taken care of, she knelt beside me. "My Cam," she whispered. "When I saw it was you—" She paused and wiped her eyes. "No—I won't cry and embarrass you." She smiled weakly at me.

"Yes'm," I said. I was so proud of her. She'd done exactly what the first-aid manual said. She'd cared for us one by one, the most serious first, even though I was her son. I wished there were a medal I could give her.

Eula called that one of the old ladies was feeling faint. "I'll be back," whispered Mama. She gathered up her supplies and hurried across the lawn.

The firemen had run their hoses down to a pond at the bottom of the yard, and they were pumping water from it onto the house. The rear wing was already gone. For a moment it seemed as if they might save the rest, but flames burst from a gable window, and they shouted that the whole attic was burning.

In the excitement, the three of us were left alone on the blankets. Jed reached over and touched my hand. "You okay, Cam?"

"I think so," I said. "Are you?"

"Bent, maybe . . . but not broke."

Tal was on my other side. "Are you okay?" I said.

He wiped his nose. "I'm awful sorry, Cam. I . . . I just wanted to be a dictator."

"Why did you want that?"

"I don't know. I was just so . . . lonely. And ashamed of things. . . ."

I remembered him lying deserted in the tower. "You don't have to be lonely," I said. "I'm your friend."

Tal blinked up at the sky. It was late afternoon now. Soon it would rain. Sparks from the fire glittered against the coming clouds. "Thank you," he said.

Shouting, the firemen fell back from the building. The blaze was beyond their control. They turned their hoses on the surrounding trees. As we watched, the outline of the house began to tremble. One side gave way and then the other. Sending up a huge cloud of sparks, it collapsed on itself.

When the ashes had settled and the yard was silent again, the old folks turned to Henry Cawley. "What's going to happen to us?" they said.

I got up with my blanket wrapped around me. "Listen," I said, getting their attention. "We got plenty of room at the Arbor. You all can come stay with us!"

Eula put her hands on her hips and gave me her astonished expression. She turned to Cawley, expecting a quick refusal, but he just looked grateful. "Perhaps, Mrs. Bethune, until we can construct a new facility . . . ?"

Breaking into a grin, she raised her arm to the old people and started for the car. "Y'all don't just stand there!" she roared. "Supper's waiting!"

ON AUGUST TWENTY-FIFTH
Daddy liberated Paris.

I was the first to hear the news over the radio. I
ran through the house, shouting it out to everybody.
The old ladies were in the parlor reading mysteries;
the men were out back hoeing in the victory garden. I
found Jed on the front porch swing with Miss Cornelia, the lady who'd welcomed him that Sunday at the
Church of the Wilderness. She wasn't living at the

Arbor like the other old people, but she visited almost every day. "Jed!" I yelled. "They did it! They made it to Paris!"

"Who did?"

"Our *boys*. The United States Army! Daddy!"

"Hoo-*ray*!" He threw out his arms and kissed Miss Cornelia. He was doing a lot of that these days. He let her go and got to his feet. "I *knew* old Pat would make it!"

Someone struck up "God Bless America" on the piano. It was Eula. Everybody crowded into the living room and began to sing with her. Jed pulled out his harmonica. He started to play, then decided to conduct us instead. I thought he looked grand up there—like Uncle Sam himself, leading the country.

We cheered when it was over. Eula struck another chord and called out, " 'America the Beautiful'!" She sounded the first notes, but the old folks were suddenly silent. They were looking toward the front hall. I turned around and saw Henry Cawley standing there. With him were Reverend Healey, Miss Airie Mitchell, and Mr. and Mrs. Spindale.

"We were in the car when we heard about the victory," he said. "A song of praise is just what's called for!"

The old people relaxed and smiled. "Less'n three months," said Jeddah. "That's all it took our boys!"

"A true miracle," said Reverend Healey. "Normandy to Paris in less than ninety days."

"Absolutely," said Cawley, beaming at us. He put his hands in his vest pockets and grew serious. "You are no doubt wondering why I have brought this delegation of distinguished Pinehill citizens here today. The answer is a simple one: I have asked them to be members of an advisory committee for the Cawley Home. Their role will be to help me plan our new facility."

Oh, Lord, I thought, what kind of place will it be with that bunch planning it? Maybe it would be fine, but I still felt suspicious of everything Mr. Cawley did. I felt like it was my duty.

Reverend Healey was nodding kindly to the old people. "My friends," he said in a rolling voice, "we want to discover firsthand your deepest needs and desires. Is there anything we can give you that will bring you fulfillment? You have only to ask, and it is yours."

Jed winked at Miss Cornelia and raised his hand. "Double beds," he said. Miss Cornelia gave a scandalized squeal. Eula started playing the National Anthem as fast as she could.

On the last chorus, Mama came in through the front door. Her hair was curling around her face. Her cheeks were bright, like she'd been running. "Did you hear?" she cried. "Did you hear the news?"

"He made it, Mama!" I said.

"Indeed he did," said Reverend Healey. "And it comes as a sign that the war is almost over."

163

Mama leaned against the archway to the hall. She pushed the hair back from her cheeks. Her fingers were shaking. "I can't believe it," she said. "It's been so long!"

I walked through the crowd to her. All I knew to say was, "Mama." She pulled my head to her chest.

"He'll be coming *home*," she whispered.

Not caring that everyone was watching, I put my arms around her. I felt so grateful. My mother had come back to me, and soon my father would too. The pieces of my life had been as scattered as the ships and flags on Charlie's map of the war. Now, one by one, I was finding them.

Mr. Cawley cleared his throat. "I would like to take this opportunity," he said in a respectful voice, "to publicly thank one of Pinehill's finest young women." He gestured to Mama, but he was aiming his words directly at the members of his committee. "I refer of course to Bess Reed. Over these last months she has given tirelessly of her time and talents to help the residents of the Cawley Home. She is a dedicated Christian, a skilled nurse—and a young wife about whom there has *never* been a breath of scandal."

Someone began to clap slowly. It was Jeddah. The old folks added to it. Soon the Spindales and even Airie Mitchell had no choice but to join in. In a moment the whole room was applauding.

Mama smiled tearfully and thanked them. From

the piano Eula called out, "This song always makes me think of Bess." Striking the keys, she sang, " 'Car-o-lina moon, keep shi-i-ning—' " We all picked it up. " '—Shi-ning on the one who waits for me—' "

I slipped out to the front porch and sat on the steps by myself. Louise was lying on the other side of the drive in the shade of the pine trees. She flopped her tail lazily against the grass when she saw me. J.W. was farther down the slope, chasing a grasshopper.

I thought back over all that had happened. Three months . . . from that wild dog on the trail to Hitler in the tower. Not much time for so many battles.

I did the best I could. No hero—still Daddy'll be proud.

Bet your boots.

Leonard Todd grew up in Greenville, South Carolina, not far from the mountains in which *The Best-Kept Secret of the War* takes place. After graduation from Yale College and the Yale School of Art and Architecture, he received a Fulbright Scholarship for two years of independent study in France. His short stories and articles have appeared in *Cosmopolitan, Travel & Leisure,* American Heritage's *Americana,* and other magazines.

A designer as well as a writer, he is the author of *Trash Can Toys & Games* (Viking Press), a guide to constructing toys from objects that are normally discarded. The toys he designed for the book were exhibited in a one-man show at the American Museum of Natural History. He also designed the layout for this book, his first novel.

Leonard Todd lives in New York City, where he is on the board of directors of Volunteer Services for Children. He is currently at work on a screenplay and a second novel.